The Bishop

DAVID HELWIG

VIKING

VIKING

Penguin Books Canada Limited,
2801 John Street, Markham, Ontario, Canada L3R 1B4

Penguin Books,
Harmondsworth, Middlesex, England

Viking Penguin Inc.,
40 West 23rd Street, New York, New York 10010 U.S.A.

Penguin Books Australia Ltd.,
Ringwood, Victoria, Australia

Penguin Books (N.Z.) Ltd.,
Private Bag, Takapuna, Auckland 9, New Zealand

First published by Penguin Books Canada Limited, 1986

Typeset by Jay Tee Graphics Ltd.
Printed and bound in the United States of America

Canadian Cataloguing in Publication Data

Helwig, David, 1938-
The bishop

ISBN 0-670-80746-X

I. Title.

PS8515.E48B57 1986 C813'.54 C85-099359-8
PR9199.3.H43B57 1986

for Bill,
who took me to church

The Arctic sections of this book contain material derived from a number of documentary sources, particularly Knud Rasmussuen's *Intellectual Culture of the Iglulik Eskimos.* I am grateful to W.J. Barnes, Brian Jackson, Lisa Miller and David Lewis Stein for expert advice in matters liturgical, theological and musical.

for Bill,
who took me to church

The Arctic sections of this book contain material derived from a number of documentary sources, particularly Knud Rasmussuen's *Intellectual Culture of the Iglulik Eskimos*. I am grateful to W.J. Barnes, Brian Jackson, Lisa Miller and David Lewis Stein for expert advice in matters liturgical, theological and musical.

One

She is laughing, something to do with the hands, Henry is unsure what, but perhaps it doesn't matter. Rose is laughing, and he sees her teeth, odd, private, startling. Other parts of the face, eyes, lips, have a known value, we study them for secrets, but then the mouth opens in laughter, and the row of bone soldiers comes to attention and vanishes. We join the laughter, or look away. Henry cannot laugh, too much of his face is paralyzed, and to look away costs more than he has, so he stares at the teeth in their flash of laughter. Something to do with the hands. Henry no longer knows where his hand ends and the world begins. His left hand is the burden of his right, and when he sees it, he doesn't know that it is his. Perhaps at death the whole body becomes like that, an innocent burden, flaccid and estranged. What he has done with the hands must have caught Rose off balance, for she is a kind woman, and it is thought cruel to laugh at invalids. Not that Henry minds; the soul may be mirthful at the abandonment of what it no longer owns. Henry is one half of a man carrying the other half, and yet the portion that lacks power and feeling is not dead. Blood flows to it; the flesh is in full health; the hair grows; but it is the victim of a blockade, the victim of a war of attrition. No news comes.

A society without the voice of God. The muscles will deteriorate to jelly. His one hand bears the other hand as its burden.

She is laughing. They sit at the table and he is aware of every atom of light that touches her skin. The light comes from the window, bright summer sun that makes the glass vibrate, makes every tiny imperfection a kind of jewel, an edge of vividness where the sunlight cuts itself into the eye. One day he will read in St. John of the Cross that the self ought to be a perfect transparency, invisible, something the light of God shines through. Yet in this glass, the tiny flecks and whorls are glittering and lovely. Amelia is laughing, and her hands are cupped on the table in front of her, poised and still and proper, as she always tries to be with him, for she is afraid that she will do something wrong and lose his love, and he cannot convince her that she never will. She will never lose his love. She is laughing, and he notices her teeth, the odd unevenness where, on the left side, beside the canine, she has, by some genetic freak, an extra incisor. As she laughs, he feels the privacy of her teeth, and the care with which she holds her hands. The roundness of the palm. Once at the fall fair, she wanted to go to the gipsy who read palms, but he wouldn't let her; it seemed dangerous and he felt it was an insult to God. The future is in God's hands.

There is a fly buzzing over the glass of the window, the sun coming through his wings. They are like stained glass. She is laughing, and the light catches the high-domed forehead and makes him feel the shape of the bones underneath. He is aware of everything, her ears, her tongue that he sees for just a moment between the teeth as she laughs. He reaches out to put his hand in her hands as they lie cupped on the table, and she clasps it tight. He sees the dark arm of his suit on the worn oilcloth of the table; it was the suit that had made her laugh. When she asked why he was wearing his suit, he said that it seemed right because he was coming to ask her to marry him, and she laughed suddenly, and for the first moment, the laughter seemed the outburst of a kind of terror, but then she met his eyes, and the fear was gone. She hasn't said yes to him; she hasn't said anything, but he knows from the way she clings to his hand that it is what she wants, what she has waited for and feared wouldn't happen. The sunlight is warm as it comes from the window and lies in a square at the edge of the table where the oilcloth is rubbed through, but her hands are cold and she hangs onto him with a fierce determination as if, without his hand to hold, she might drown. He is pulling her back from the cold water, from the past, from the awkward, tilted little house where she lives with her mother and her sister, everything rubbed bare by poverty and the emptiness where her father should have been. It is Henry who will save her; she has always known it, has watched him, even when she was a little girl and he taught Sunday school once in her class. She looked for him every Sunday when he played at the park with the band, until the day they met there and walked together. These things she saved to tell him — how she had seen him and waited until somehow she could find a place to speak. Now they will be married and live together forever, and that moment will always be his, when he said he had put on his suit to propose, and she laughed, out of shock and pleasure and the silliness of it. What he wants her to know is how he can be silly with her, how he can be weak and foolish. With her he is safe.

She is watching him now, waiting for him to speak, and he wants to tell her this, that they are both safe now, that they are together in the hands of God, but he wants to tell her without speaking, only with the way his eyes hold her eyes and her lips and her hair. She sits straight. Her hair is fine, and her eyes are dark, with golden flecks. Henry tries to imagine what God is thinking as he watches the two of them staring at each other, their hands locked, and he thinks that perhaps God is laughing.

Sunlight is an emanation of the laughter of God. Henry walks across the tundra towards the mission. He has walked fifteen miles to meet the people at their summer camp, and he has stayed with them for two days.

The sunlight over the tundra is brilliant now, but last night it rained, and he took his bedroll into the tent with Ishakak and his wife. He slept only inches away from them, and he could hear every sound. In the morning the fish came, and all the Inuit ran into the water and began to spear the shining bodies of the arctic char. Henry started to hike back down the river.

The arctic air is brilliant, and he feels that he is breathing the light, as if every mouthful of air is a small explosion in his throat and his lungs. His sealskin boots make a damp sound as he wades through the wet mosses and plants of the tundra, and there are flowers all around his feet.

Henry looks at the flowers that grow beside each soggy footprint, the pure colours, the transparency of the petals. When he gets closer to the mission, he will pick a bouquet of them for Amelia. They are like grace, these white and yellow and purple wildflowers, unexpected, undeserved. He will take them to her, a little gift from the surface of his love.

He makes his way down a small hill, and beside him he hears the teeming rush of the river waters as they fall, and when he gets to the bottom, he walks to the edge of the river to kneel on a rock and drink. The water is so cold it stings his mouth. Men and women stand in the water with their spears, catching fish as they have caught them for a thousand years. Henry rises to his feet and begins to walk. He loves the way his muscles respond as his legs carry him over the tundra and the patches of bare rock. He loves the way the sun falls on the high cliffs to his right, bringing out the multitude of colours. Sunlight is the laughter of God.

When he is close to the mission, he bends, and carefully he picks the flowers, trying to find the largest, the most perfect blossoms. With the bouquet in his hand, he continues down the trail to the white clapboard building. At the Hudson's Bay store, a dog is barking. Henry opens the door. She has been looking towards the blue of the inlet. She turns towards him, and he is stunned. He holds out the flowers and he can't understand the look on her face as she stares at them, and then her eyes turn to the table. On the table is a bouquet almost identical to the one in his hand, flowers that she has brought in from a walk. They both look at the two bouquets, and they laugh together.

Rose was shocked at her own laughter, but it had caught her off guard when the bishop had taken hold of her hand and tried to place it in the sling that hung from his shoulder to support his paralyzed hand and arm. He had lost sensation in his left hand at the time of the stroke, and he was unable, for a moment, to tell his insensible hand from hers. When she realized why he was tugging her hand towards him, she couldn't help it, the laughter had exploded. His eyes looked puzzled as they caught hers, and she was unable to explain, except to mumble something about the hands and put his paralyzed left hand back in the sling where it belonged. Aphasia. Hemiplegia. They sounded like minor cities of the Roman Empire, places that Paul or one of the other apostles might have visited. Paul's Letter to the Aphasians. Aphasians, Chapter 1, Verse 1. *My mouth is stopped and cannot utter speech.*

She must control herself. It was no joking matter, the bishop lying mute with half his body useless. Probably he should be in a convalescent hospital somewhere, but he had insisted on being brought back here to his rooms at the top of the house by the cathedral. The diocesan offices were downstairs, and when he first arrived here, translated from his former diocese, the bishop had made little jokes about living over the shop, and they had reconstructed the top level of the house as a small apartment. The bishop would answer the door and the phone at all hours of the day and night, and it was difficult for the rest of the staff to be anything less than wholly committed when he was always waiting for them to arrive, and still at work after they left. At first, there had been a little uneasiness felt by the cathedral clergy because the bishop insisted on living in their backyard, more or less, and wished to preach and celebrate communion at the cathedral more often than was conventional. But it was impossible to resent anything Henry did for long. The wide, bright, nervous smile won Rose over to him the day they met, and now she would have done anything for him. He made her feel at rest in her solitude, as he was at rest in his. She had heard women wonder how a man who was still handsome in his seventies could have remained alone, a widower, for forty years, but Rose felt that perhaps she understood, that the man was so open to every person he came near that he had only once needed a spouse to share his privacy. He was in the world, and he was alone with God. He was at peace, and working near him had led Rose towards a serenity she had never thought to possess.

The nurse would be back in thirty minutes from her afternoon break.

"Is there anything else you want?" Rose asked.

The eyes met hers and were still. He needed nothing. His hand didn't move towards the pad where he wrote messages. He seldom used it, and was apparently content to be locked inside his body, imprisoned in silence. At first when you looked at his face, it was so close to normal that you expected words, speech, the familiar smile, the familiar voice, but no smile came, no speech, and the paralyzed side of the face *was*, you gradually noticed, different. She tried not to stare at him, but there was a need to know him as he was now, *Henry, our bishop,* who had given her peace, who had accepted, or excused, even her loopy sense of humour.

It was Rose who had found him, after the stroke. She had ridden her bicycle to work, as she always did in good weather, and in spite of the fact that she had taken the long way, along the water, she was the first to arrive. The door was locked, which was strange, for by this hour, the bishop was always down in his office. She let herself in; the rooms were quiet, and she began to be afraid, called out, got no answer but the tiny echo of her voice. Rose went up the stairs, that day, with superstitious care; she wanted to race up, but made herself walk slowly from step to step. The second floor was empty, one of the office doors open, and through the door she saw a window and outside, the sun shining on green leaves; a sparrow flew away from the tree and out of sight.

Rose began to make her way, step by step, to the top floor. She felt that if she walked carefully, that if she put her foot firmly on each step, it would be an act of faith, and he would be alive when she reached him. This careful walk was a kind of prayer. The bedroom door was closed.

She knocked and waited a moment, thinking, what if he died because she was dilatory in reaching him?

When she opened the door, the body, at first, looked quite still, but as she crossed the room, she saw the contortion of the face, a Halloween mask on one side, a grimace of pain or distress on the other, and one of the eyes opened and saw her.

"Bishop?" she said.

He said nothing. The eye stared at her.

"Bishop . . . Henry."

She had never called him by his name before, except in prayer, *Henry, our bishop*, but there was some despairing need to reach him. One of his hands moved, and she reached out and took it in her own. It was pale and slender, with long delicate fingers, and looked odd in the grasp of her big hard hand, with its broken nails and cuts and stains and calluses, the stub where she was missing the top two joints of one of her fingers. She grasped his hand tightly. The one open eye seemed not so much to look at her as to search for her, as if she were far off from him, a figure lost in darkness.

Now, after his stay in hospital, both his eyes were open, though one eyelid drooped heavily and gave him a wary look, like some careful French *boulevardier*, Rose couldn't help thinking, surveying the new shipment of country girls at his favourite brothel. An unsuitable image, but she couldn't resist noticing it, that he looked oddly raffish with the partial paralysis of his face. She was tempted to tell him so, but she couldn't catch enough from the responses of his eyes to dare the sort of joke she had made with him before. Odd, the eyes. You stared into the eyes of those you were close to, and you saw, or thought you saw, some deep communication, love or desire or trust, but when the eyes were on their own, when there was no other way to communicate, they became dangerously unclear in their meaning. They might be saying anything. Hate and love could suddenly look the same.

On the table beside the Bishop's bed was the box that Rose had made for him which contained his Bible and prayer book. It was made of mahogany, and it always slightly annoyed her to see it, since mahogany was a wood she didn't particularly like, but she had decided one weekend to make it, and she had no other hardwoods in the workshop and hadn't had the patience to wait until she could acquire some. Perhaps she should make a replacement. She had cherry now, and even some pieces of apple wood that she could use for ornament. She'd burned out the motor on her table-saw trying to mill the apple out of a small trunk she'd picked up. Bicycling past, Rose had seen it lying by the side of the road where someone had cut down the tree, and she'd borrowed a small station wagon that belonged to Gordon Budge, the cathedral organist, to pick it up and take it to the workshop where it lay drying for the next few months. It was difficult to work, stone-hard and with a tendency to split, but beautiful, a rich pale brown wood with shades of burnt sienna, and gold, and a dark colour that was almost purple.

It was foolish of her to have been so impatient about

making the box, but some great access of affection for the bishop had struck her when she woke that Saturday morning, remembering his smile as he had left for a short trip the night before. The brightness of his eyes when he smiled. The ease with which he sang out, "Good-night, Rose. God bless you." She had always thought of sainthood as stricken, solitary, a kind of incapacity as much as a blessing, and she had seen too much false clerical cheer, hypocrisy masquerading as beatitude, but the music of this man's voice was true. So she had wakened that dim winter morning, with the clouds close and threatening snow, and she had felt that she must make him something. She had climbed on her bike and ridden to the diocesan centre, which had her workshop in the basement as well as his apartment at the top. That was another of his decisions that had caused a stir around the diocese. The building where Rose had previously had her woodworking shop had been sold, and she'd mentioned in passing that she'd have to rent a new location. Henry had decided on the instant that the basement of the diocesan centre was the perfect place. She could pay the rent, he insisted, by doing repairs on the cathedral and the other church buildings when they were needed.

There was an old galvanized sink in the corner of the basement, and beside it, Rose kept a kettle. As soon as she arrived that morning, she made coffee, and while she drank it, she sketched a box with one compartment for the Bible and another for the prayer book. She glued and clamped two pieces of one-by-six mahogany side by side to make a foot in width, and then went out to buy the hinges while the glue dried. She would plane the mahogany down to three-eighths so the box wasn't ungainly. Rose puzzled over the question of a lock, and concluded that the bishop would think it wrong to put a lock on any box designed to hold the word of God. It would delight him to think that someone wished to go away with his Bible or prayer book. In fact, he would willingly have given away any of his possessions, and it was only the insistence of the other diocesan officers that convinced him to lock the doors of the house at night. His explanation was that he was sure to lose his key and get locked out, but that was only an excuse. He hated the thought of being distrustful. He was one of the lilies of the field. He made her think of the desert monk who, after he had been robbed, ran after the thief to give him some object he'd missed.

Just what were the lilies of the field? She realized that the phrase had summoned, not quite into the mind, but into a suburb of the mind, a picture of Easter lilies growing wild somewhere. They were horrible flowers, with white embalmed flesh, an image of all the worst possibilities of death. When she had found the bishop after his stroke, the skin of his face had been white like that, the transparent white of the blocks of paraffin that her mother used to melt to make a wax seal at the top of her jars of jam and jelly. When it was put on top of the jar, it was half transparent, and you could see the dark colour of the jam underneath. She remembered the trick of getting the wax off the jar without spilling too many pieces in the jam; you cut one careful line across the middle of the wax and lifted out the two semicircles. Rose had tried to teach Joanne, who was awkward with her hands and could never learn; Joanne always ended up having to pick pieces of wax out of the strawberry preserve, though she always did it so daintily, so gracefully, that it seemed this must be the proper way for the thing to be done.

Whatever the lilies of the field were, they surely weren't Easter lilies, or anything like them. Orange lilies, perhaps, which grew wild by the side of the road every summer. Or daisies or black-eyed Susans. Something that loved the sun and spread prodigally. Prodigal: it had never occurred to her before that Jesus' teaching had been a praise of prodigality. One must not be too prudent with the one talent. The father's prodigality, in its own way, equalled the son's.

The creation of the box that weekend, working impatiently in mahogany, missing Sunday service, working late into the night and getting up early Monday morning, was a kind of prodigality. Yes. She was pleased that she had done it that way. Rose had given the box to the bishop when he arrived back Monday morning. He hadn't spoken, had only reached out to take it, and looked at her and smiled, then turned and walked up the stairs with the box in his hands. He didn't need to speak; she knew what he felt.

Rose turned away from the bed and went to the window. In the street beneath, a tiny blonde girl pushed her child, who had the same pale soft hair, in a stroller. The young mother was smiling as she walked, and with her fresh complexion and bright hair, she looked like a creation of the summer sun. She moved out of sight behind the rough grey bark of the maple that grew at the side of the house. To the right, but out of Rose's line of vision, was the cathedral. Though Rose couldn't see it, she felt its presence. It frightened her at times, its bulk, and the way it confronted earth and sky, its impersonality, and the two thousand years of history that it embodied. What she liked best were its devious ways: the underground passage that led from the bishop's house to the maze of offices, one end reaching a wooden door in Rose's workshop, the other a set of stone steps beneath a stained glass window commemorating the piety of a nineteenth century marine provisioner; the room within a room that was the choir library, appearing at first to be a closet, but when the door was opened, discovered to be a long thin room with windows at each end and a multitude of shelves; the short passage to the hidden door which led Gordon to the organ console, out of sight of the congregation; the abruptly turning hallways with their unexpected windows, multiple doors, closets and stairways; the huge basement carved out of stone, with its areas of civilization, storage for things long forgotten, and beyond, the dusty chaos where wild cats lived and bred.

Where the stone stairway from the bishop's passage rose, there was an empty room with one tall slender window, and here the bishop had asked her to build shelves and chests for a cathedral archive so the books and documents that were now stored in the basement, bequests from church members, libraries of early bishops, might be safely stored and perhaps catalogued. She hadn't yet begun the work. Soon she must measure the room and begin some sketches.

It was one of the days when the Lord was with Thy Spirit, and Norman had escaped through the Pipe Hole to the corner where, with his back against the stone, he could watch both ways, and he would know if Thy Spirit was coming. Thy Spirit had never found him yet, but on days when the Lord was with Thy Spirit, Norman could find comfort nowhere else.

He had to hide from everyone, even Chappie and Bill. Chappie was the Sex-Tom and Bill was his helper. They brought Norman in the first time, to carry chairs, but they didn't know he was here now, and he had to make sure they didn't find him. The Pipe Hole that led to his corner was tight and dusty, and Norman knew that no one would come here. It was here he kept Elvis and the dry stiff body of the messenger pigeon he had found lying in the street. The pigeon had smelled for a while, and white worms had slimed out of it, so he had left it further along the Pipe Hole until it got hard and dry and the worms went away. Elvis was painted on cloth, and he was taller than Norman. Glory got him to hang on her wall, and when she was gone, Norman went for the white cat and he had taken the picture of Elvis to help him remember Glory. There would be a time when Glory came back, when she'd be to the father and the son and the Holey Ghost. The Holey Ghost was a puzzle. Whether he lived in a hole, or whether he was all full of holes. And why Glory would be to him. But then Norman didn't understand why Glory would be to his father either. She would be to Norman because Norman had always loved her.

Sometimes when he remembered Glory, it was like dreaming, except in dreaming, he was always scared, but he was scared too when he remembered the white cat. Glory loved the cat, and she loved Norman. She would kneel in front of him when he was mad, and she would beg him to be good. C'mon, Norman, c'mon, she'd say, and she'd give him a little smile. And later on she'd feed him Kentucky Fried Chicken with her own fingers. She'd pick up the white cat and stroke it and clean its ears. That cat was her baby. Glory couldn't have any because they gave her the operation, so she had that cat for her baby instead.

Why would she be to his father? Norman's father wouldn't talk to him. Once he took Norman out in the country, and Norman fell in the water and almost drowned, and after that his father wouldn't ever talk to him. Why would Glory be to him?

When Norman found the messenger pigeon on the street, dead, he picked it up to be a present for Glory. It was Chappie who told him about the messenger pigeons, how there used to be millions and millions and millions, but they were gone now. But sometimes Norman would see one of the pigeons coming down to the shed where they sat under the edge of the roof, and he'd know that this one was a messenger pigeon. So he was saving the dead messenger pigeon to give to Glory when she came back to be to him.

One way from his corner in the Pipe Hole was the house with the loud machines, and the other way was the church. Sometimes he thought that Thy Spirit might come from both ways at once.

If Thy Spirit started to come, Norman knew how to run to the curving stairs, and then there were more stairs that went inside the wall, and at the top, you could see down into the whole church with everything shining and clean the way Chappie and Bill kept it, the light coming through the coloured windows with pictures of Jesus in his long dress. Sometimes Norman sat up there, where no one could see him, and listened to them talking about Thy Spirit and the Angels and Dark Angels. If he peeked down, everyone was small.

Norman started to crawl down the Pipe Hole out of his corner. Thy Spirit wouldn't come for him now the singing had started. He crawled without breathing to keep the dust out of his mouth, then stopped when he was almost at the end of the Pipe Hole and listened for sounds. He had to be careful that they didn't catch him. He'd never find another place like this. There was no unexpected noise. He got his head out of the Pipe Hole and looked. To get down to the floor, he had to bend his body tightly together, lying on his back and then slowly turning so his feet could go down first.

Norman was going to the Cat Room first. He walked

slowly when he got close to the room, putting each foot down softly. If the cat heard him coming, it would scramble away before he could see it, and that was bad luck. Seeing the cat was good luck, and if he could ever touch it, that would be the best luck, but the cat never let him.

When he was close to the doorway, he went even slower, his hands pressed against the legs of his pants; his legs started to tremble and he could feel it in his fingers. He knew that the cat was trembling too, softly under the fur, the way cats do. He remembered how the white cat had been trembling. Sometimes he believed that this was the same cat, but in different fur, and that it had come back looking for Norman.

Henry waited impatiently for night, when they would leave him alone in the darkness. They thought there was something ominous, something dangerous, about leaving him in the night, but he was frightened of nothing. Everything that could frighten him had already happened long ago.

Rose had come to see him when the nurse brought his dinner. Her squat, powerful figure was a pleasure to him; he didn't have the illusion, held by some of those in the diocesan office, that she was cold and remote; he understood how easily touched she was. Sometimes he thought she was in love with him, in some distant, harmless way, and Henry did not discourage it. Love came in many forms, and he had learned how few of these should be avoided. He took no pride in her feeling. It sprang from no virtue in him, and it was impersonal really, a need and a power exercising itself because he was close and tried to encourage love of all kinds. Rose had never told him her story, and yet he knew somehow that there was one, a life left hanging, a half-tragedy, something uncompleted that would never find an earthly resolution, like a melody that has been interrupted on a difficult chord, an echo of possibilities always there. Dear Rose. He would never know her story now unless the dead were allowed such secrets; but it hardly mattered. He could hear the echo of it in her voice. There was something in the touch of her hands that told him all he needed to know. In her impatience. The Bible box she rushed to make over a weekend, in a wood she didn't like, because she had some urgent loving need to have it completed and in his hand. When love gripped her, she was shaken too deeply to have any control. Dear Rose, he would say to her if he had a voice, I have loved you very much for the gusty weather of your attack on the world.

The room was almost dark now except for a little light from the doorway, beyond which one of the nurses, who minded him as if he were a child, dozed on a couch. Now and then he would wake and find her looking down at him. She surveyed him at regular intervals during the night, like a nightwatchman overseeing a yard full of industrial goods, to make sure that no one had broken in and stolen anything valuable, though the only robber was the guest Henry expected and desired. There were moments when he was frightened of death, when a cold chill from under the earth seized him, but he stared down nothingness, non-existence, and sooner or later it would retreat and leave him with his immeasurable hopes. He had never before tried seriously to understand how human souls might come together in the other world. Was it too simple to think that his father would, as always, shake his hand firmly and yet with a certain reticence, a respected and decent man of his era? God surely had more imagination than that. Yet Henry would be satisfied with that, the mere thing, the lost details, to look his father in the face, shake his hand. And how would he meet Amelia? He would leave that to God. In God's hands. Who was he to assume that God chose to resolve for men what was left unresolved from their life on earth? Would he be satisfied to go on with what she had been to him and he to her? An eternity of something missed. Though Jesus said there would be no marriage and giving in marriage, and without marriage, and its hopes and bonds, perhaps their love could be perfect. Perhaps there would be no individuals at all, only the radiance of God's pure love without the particularity of its embodiments. He would miss them, human beings, but he'd had many years of them, and he could do without if that was what was to be.

A few generations earlier, he might have pondered and feared damnation, but he wasn't much interested in hell. Its existence, if it was a fact, did not need study. Pain and suffering were easy enough to understand, but fulfillment, completion, those were things that could hold the mind forever, just to imagine them, just to think of the rainbow of possibilities. That wisdom might be completed. Delight. Beauty. It seemed to him that each night he discovered yet more paths to follow towards the face of God. Perhaps in time, he would find the path where he could meet Amelia and walk with her.

The corner of window that he could see from his bed was dim. The texture of the wall outside, made vivid and three-dimensional by the setting sun a few minutes before, was flattening into darkness. Few churches had evensong any more; the old evening hymns were unused. *Abide with me, fast falls the eventide.* In the old days of the brass band, his friend Fred liked to play a ragtime version of the hymn. Henry would try to imitate him, but he wasn't good at it, though he played traditional music better than Fred. Once Henry's mother heard him trying to play jazz and said she disliked to hear him play "that darky music."

Alice-Alice called out to him from the parlour.

"Henry, come and play duets."

Sundays, after service, he and his sister would go to the parlour and play sacred pieces together.

"Not many, today," he said. "We're playing at the park this afternoon."

There had been some discussion in the family about the suitability of band concerts on Sunday afternoon.

"It's an innocent pastime," his father had said. "It gives people a harmless pleasure. Henry could do much worse."

His father could balance propriety and an easy acceptance of the world. Henry wondered if he would be able to do the same. He opened the cornet case, and put the mouthpiece in the shining silver horn. Alice began to play "O Jesus I Have Promised," and he put the instrument to his lips and joined her. He knew the tune so well that he didn't have to read the music and transpose from concert pitch. The words sang in his head:

I shall not fear the battle
If thou art by my side,
Nor wander from the pathway
If thou wilt be my guide.

How hard Reverend Dennison made it sound when Henry told him that he wanted to study and be ordained.

"How was it last night?" Alice-Alice asked when they reached the end of the hymn. He wasn't surprised that they were thinking of the same thing. The whole family was aware that he had gone to speak to the minister, and in church this morning when Reverend Dennison had made oblique reference to those who sought ordination, they all knew he was referring to Henry.

"He made it sound hard," Henry said. "He made it sound awfully hard."

"It wouldn't be so hard," she said, "if he had a wife."

"Catholic priests don't have wives. None of them."

"But they're RC. It's not the same."

Alice-Alice wanted him to show an interest in her

friend Louise. Henry was shy with girls; he never knew what to say to them; he didn't much like Louise. Mother told him not to worry about being shy; when the right girl came along, he wouldn't be. She said his father used to be very shy until he met her. It was just a matter of waiting for the right girl.

Reverend Dennison asked him about self-abuse. Henry said he thought he had it under control. Reverend Dennison didn't ask about dreams, just advised Henry to pray and then began to talk about the loneliness of the life of a clergyman, how much was demanded of him by everyone, how he was expected to be a better man than anyone else. Henry was disappointed that they didn't talk more about God. That was why he went, because he felt that with the minister he would feel free to talk about God in a way he wasn't with anyone else. Now and then, with Alice-Alice or his parents, he might say something, just a word or two, but he couldn't say anything to Fred. Fred would have thought talking about God outside of church in bad taste. He didn't think Henry should try to be ordained. Sometimes it was hard with the band; the time they took the train to Toronto, for instance. If Henry admitted he didn't like their dirty jokes, they'd think he was odd. They already teased him about girls. It wasn't wrong that he didn't like dirty jokes.

Alice-Alice was turning the pages of the hymn book.

"Just one more," he said to his sister. "I don't want to lose my lip."

"Are you playing a solo?"

" 'Carnival of Venice'."

"With the triple-tonguing?"

"Of course."

"Maybe you shouldn't play any more. 'Carnival of Venice' is hard."

"One more is all right. It will get me warmed up."

"The girls all watch you, you know, when you're playing a solo. You look so handsome."

"Don't be silly. Just pick a hymn."

She started to play "Who Are These Like Stars Appearing." He had to watch the music and transpose; he didn't like that as well. It made his chest and his lip tense because he was thinking about the intervals. It was like thinking when you tried to pray. When he had prayed with Reverend Dennison, he couldn't stop thinking, and somehow God disappeared. When he went to divinity school, there would be men to whom he could say these things. He would be free to speak with his whole mind.

Now in God's most holy place
Blest they stand before his face.

There *was* a girl who watched him. She was always there, and he could feel her eyes on him. Would she come to hear him play "Carnival of Venice"? He triple-tongued the last few notes of the hymn, just to prove to himself that it was there.

His sister smiled at him.

"Don't let Mother hear you doing that," she said.

The sun was a bright swirl in the white curtains on the windows. The material moved just a little in a breeze that came from an open window somewhere in the back of the house. Henry put the cornet back in its case, the silver fitting into the blue velvet form. He would play in the same dark suit he had worn to church.

"I'm going to walk down to the park now," he said.

"I'll pick up Louise, and we'll walk down together."

Henry didn't want Alice-Alice and Louise to come. He didn't want his parents to come. He knew who would be there watching him, and he wanted to play for her alone. It was all in a moment that he knew all these things, knew that with her he wouldn't be shy. He knew so many things in that moment, and he walked out the door and down the street to the park on the edge of the lake as if he moved through a new kind of sunlight.

In one of the high park elms, he saw a family of young squirrels, dashing through the branches. The elms spread like green parasols over the fresh grass of the park.

Henry saw the figures of the other band members in the scatter of sun and shade around the bandstand, in their dark suits, one or two with their jackets hung on a chair or the rail of the bandstand, their white shirts striped by the braces that held up their trousers. He stopped. He felt as if he were on the far side of a glass wall. In a moment he would walk through it and be one of the group, and he would smile and laugh with them and warm up his lip and sort his music, but now he saw them with an odd detachment in which there seemed to be some hint of how God might see the world, every detail vivid, and yet far off.

No. God was not distant. If he went on thinking like that, he would end like Reverend Dennison, a man committed to an insoluble loneliness. Henry thought a kind of prayer and walked through the glass wall, and after one step forward, he was just another of the men gathered here to make music. Fred, who had taken off his coat, waved to him, and the arm was like a white flag, a flag of truce. To imitate the love of God was not to stand on the far side of a glass wall, but to walk among men as one of them.

"Henry's here," Cam Sleeth shouted out. "Now the girls will start to come."

"How's the lip?" Fred said.

"Henry's been warming it up since church with one of his girl-friends," Cam said. He made a crude noise through his mouthpiece.

Henry took the cornet out of his case and played a few showy runs and high notes by way of an answer.

"She sure warmed you up this morning," Cam said. He wasn't to be stopped that easily.

Fred turned aside from the crowd.

"Did you talk to him?"

"Yes."

"I hope he told you to give up the whole idea and become a musician."

"He told me I'd be lonely."

Henry put the cornet in its case and set it on the stairs. He and Fred walked away from the bandstand a few paces.

Fred couldn't understand his desire to be ordained, his need for it. Fred attended church for the same reason he polished his shoes once a week and got a haircut once a fortnight. It was right. It was what one did. There seemed no point in trying to explain it to him, the longing for something one couldn't always name, for whatever it was that made all of life sing like music.

"Dennison would be lonely whatever he did. He's a poor stick."

Henry felt the same thing, but he couldn't bring himself to express disrespect for a man who had committed his life to God.

"I guess it can be a hard life," he said.

Fred sat down on one of the benches. From here the water of the lake was just visible through the thick green leaves of the trees.

"If I could play like you," Fred said, "I know what I'd do."

"You can play jazz," Henry said. "I can't."

"That's just something I fool around with."

People were arriving at the park for the concert. Once again, Henry was behind the glass wall. A Model T Ford pulled up at the edge of the park, and the Purtle family tumbled out. Mrs Purtle was carrying a hamper of food and one of the boys had a blanket to spread on the grass. Roy Purtle was in Henry's Sunday school class; he was a loud, foolish boy. Henry saw Captain Woodrow, the band conductor, striding towards the members of his band. He had a red face and round belly, but he held himself upright and marched forward with a military swing of the right arm. Under the left arm was a leather case which held his music and baton. Some of the bandsmen saw him coming, and began to arrange the chairs and music stands.

"We better get back," Henry said.

Captain Woodrow had conducted an army band in the war, and he expected military discipline from his little group of citizen musicians. He didn't get it, but most of them tried to make some kind of gesture. As Fred and Henry strolled back to the bandshell, more of the afternoon's audience drifted into the park. Henry noticed his parents with the Mackenzies, but he didn't see Alice-Alice and her friend Louise. Then, as if a lantern slide had been projected on the vivid screen of leaves, he saw the girl, the one who watched him; but in a second, the slide was changed, and she vanished. Henry stared at the shivering air where she had been.

When they got back to the bandstand, his cornet and case were gone.

"Where's my cornet?" he said.

Cam Sleeth was grinning at him.

"Probably one of your girlfriends stole it for a souvenir."

"Where did you put it?"

Cam grinned. Henry felt he would have liked to knock him down, and at the same time, he felt a childish desire to cry.

"Where did you put it?"

"In the Ladies'. Give them a jim-dandy thrill when you go in to get it."

Captain Woodrow was in his place with his music spread on the stand in front of him. More and more people were taking seats in the rows of wooden benches, or spreading blankets on the grass nearby. Henry couldn't see his sister anywhere; she was the only one he could ask to get the instrument for him. He couldn't run to his mother.

"What are you going to do?" Fred whispered.

"I don't know."

Fred was laughing.

"It's not funny."

"I can't help it."

"What am I going to do?"

"Get Captain Woodrow to make an announcement."

"Be serious. I have to get my cornet."

"Just shout 'Excuse Me' and walk in."

"I can't do that."

Captain Woodrow was looking down at Henry, frowning because he was late in taking his place. He thought Henry was getting too big for his breeches because he was playing solos now. Henry turned and walked away towards the women's washroom at the back of the bandstand. Once when they were little, Alice-Alice had tried to get him to go in with her, but he'd refused. He tried to imagine what it would be like to walk in now, what he'd see. Someone might scream and he would be arrested as a masher, and everyone would hear, and he'd never be able to study for the ministry and be ordained. There was a wooden wall built outside the door of the women's washroom so the little boys couldn't try to peek in, and as he walked by, he thought he saw a figure standing beside the door, but he was afraid to be caught staring. He couldn't make himself walk in; he'd have to ask his mother, and he'd never hear the end of that from the other members of the band. *Henry needs his mother to look after him. Is Henry's mother going on the trip with us?* He glanced back once more, desperate.

There was a figure coming towards him. A pink dress. Walking quickly. She had the cornet case in her hand. She left the shade and entered the bright sunlight and for a moment his vision blurred and he wasn't sure if she was there at all. Then she was close in front of him and the case was in his hands. She turned away, without speaking, and for a moment he stood still, unable to remember her face. He tried to remember if his fingers had touched hers, but nothing was clear any more; he wasn't even sure if their eyes had met, and yet as he turned back to the bandstand, he felt buoyant, as if he walked on waves of light that fell on the park from the midday sun.

He climbed the stairs, passed Captain Woodrow, who fussed with his scores, smiled at Cam Sleeth in the trombone section and took his seat beside Fred, who had his music on the stand ready for him.

"How did you get it?"

Henry couldn't explain. He wanted to say that a messenger from God had brought it to him, but it sounded silly, and probably it was blasphemous. He looked up from his music as he put the mouthpiece in the instrument, and hoped that he would see her, but there was no sign of her. He could see Alice-Alice and Louise in a row near the front, whispering together and looking towards him.

He knew that when he stood to play "Carnival of Venice" he would see her, and he played his way carefully and joyfully through the concert until then. Fred was playing very well, and the sound of their two instruments blended. The moment he stood for the solo, his eyes found her, off to one side, standing against a tree in her pink dress.

Something began in his mind and body as he played for her; something began and did not end.

After the concert, he avoided the others. He wanted to study this new thing. As Henry walked across the park towards the water, it was there, a voice that he could not quite hear, and he thought it might be some kind of prayer, a new never-before-known voice of inner worship that prayed itself without his will. The grass beneath his feet was not solid, but buoyant, as if the whole park were floating on the surface of the water, swinging slowly in the movement of the wind and current. The sound in his mind was like that, all gentle movement, a pure voice detached from words and syntax, a liturgy, a noteless music, which he thought he would never hear again, so that the memory of that day would always be mysterious and vivid, like something he had dreamed, bright lights and slow flying.

The sunlight was one colour dappling under the green shade of the high old trees, and another colour in the wide space over the water. Ahead of his feet was a shimmer of light where a beam of sun penetrated the thick leaves, and the shivering at the fringes was the echo of the secret prayer. He stood still, the toes of his shoes just touching the sunlight, the black, square cornet case in his right hand, a young man in a dark suit, silent and alone in this corner of the wide park, this floating island of green foliage embroidered with radiance.

The secret prayer was drawing him somewhere, and where this light came down, it was stronger, until it became a chorus of tongues, a vivid mental glossolalia, a wordless song. How did he know it was prayer? Because prayer was what he sought, and therefore must be what he attained. A thousand times in his life, he would try to remember the sound, try to achieve it again and discover if it was perhaps not prayer at all, but some malign fingering of the keys of temptation. He thought sometimes it had begun in his mouth with the triple-tonguing of "Carnival of Venice," the flesh moving too rapidly, captured by some inner glittering that was produced when cells moved too fast, the triple-tonguing that was all flash and drew her eyes to him, the glitter of Sunday sunlight on his cornet. But on that afternoon, he could only feel it as prayer, this most mysterious flower of the floating earth.

How long did he stand at the moment of sunlight? He saw himself there a long time; he saw it all as the eye of a bird or a minor angel, who watched just over the treetops, could see the two of them, and the way the space between them resonated with the same sound as buzzed in his brain, and she was still, as he was, though he would never know what music or prayer or tingle of possibility was in her mind. He would never know. He would never know. Perhaps the angel knew, who hung in the brilliant blue air above the trees and watched on God's behalf as Henry walked across the lush grass to the hill by the water, and just as he made his way down the hill, awkward in his good black shoes, he looked to his left across the smooth beach of rounded stones, and as he saw her, the prayer in his head stopped, for she was its object. The angel above perhaps turned away and wept iridescent tears from the pain of foreknowledge. Perhaps it was at that moment, when the angel looked away that the sound, the prayer, the noiseless noise in the brain stopped, and there was a huge booming gong of silence in the whole space between the water and the emptiness of the sky, an explosion of silence and light, and she was at the centre of it, her slender white legs dipped in the water where she stood, her skirt held up around her hips, her thin shoulders held very straight as she gazed across the miles of water, to where the sun glittered on tiny waves like a million cherubim turning their faces suddenly upward to praise God.

In his dark suit, carrying the black case, he looked, perhaps, like some ominous messenger, a hangman or a priest to the condemned, and now that the prayer had stopped in his brain, he was aimless, awkward, unclear where to turn next, and so once again he stood still and watched her from behind as she gazed towards the lake's horizon.

Below the short sleeves of the dress, her thin arms were bare and bent a little to hold up the edges of her skirt, catching it just lightly in her fingers, as if she might be about to dance or drop a curtsy before an antique queen. His eyes could feel the small bones of her shoulders and the delicate neck. The pale skin of her bare legs. She stood, her back to him, looking over the water. She had stood near the edge of the bandstand, her eyes watching him, still, dark, concentrated. He wanted to touch her, to see how his touch would be reflected in the eyes. He wanted to kiss the bare legs. He had never felt the skin of a woman except in dreams. He could read the shape of her bones.

The skirt was gathered forward around the curve of her hips, and then the white legs disappeared in the shining water. He watched her so intensely that he could see her ribs expand with each breath, and he thought that he might begin to laugh or cry, he couldn't tell which. "Carnival of Venice" began to play itself over again in his mind, and his tongue was faster now, the triple-tonguing was quick as light. The sound from the bell of the cornet burst in the bright air, and her eyes were there at the edge of the crowd, studying him, demanding something from him.

He stood at the bottom of the hill, in his dark suit,

the case in his hand, and he could see everything about her more and more clearly, the dark hairs that lay across her forearm. He observed the way she held her shoulders until he was holding his the same way.

If he didn't touch her, he would begin to scream, piercing screams to frighten the observing angel. But was the angel still with him? The odd tingling prayerfulness was gone. Perhaps the angel had hidden his eyes in his wing, afraid for what might happen, afraid for the thing in him that felt he must touch her lest something break. He would never know how long he stood close behind her. Time ended and time began. He was unable to see anything but the figure of the girl in front of him; he stood as she stood, his body an echo of hers. He breathed when she breathed.

When she turned towards him, his breath stopped. She looked at him, as if she had known that he would be there, as if she had known he would come and what he would feel. Her eyes understood his fear and shared it, and she walked out of the water and came towards him, his hands torn with the need to hold her body against his. Her eyes were calm, aware, as if she had the same terrible foreknowledge as the weeping angel, but accepted it. As she came towards him, out of the water, she dropped the edges of her skirt and it fell to cover her legs. She sat on a log and took up one of the white stockings that lay there. He waited. The fabric covered the small bones of her feet, her ankles. He would never forget the shape of her toe, instep, heel. One of her stockings had a hole at the end, and the round toe that showed through it held his eyes. She began to put on her shoes.

He waited. He would wait forever if need be. Tiny ripples of water spoke against pebbles, small voices of the lake. In the distance he could see a fishing boat, long and wide, with a low cabin.

I will make you fishers of men,
fishers of men, fishers of men,
I will make you fishers of men,
If you follow me.

He hummed the tune, remembered how he had seen her once when he was teaching Sunday school. He had seen her somewhere else, before that; perhaps in dreams.

She was fastening the strap of her shoe. She was slow and awkward, and her fingers were shaking. He put down the cornet case and went and knelt on the stones in front of her and took the other shoe and put it on her foot and did up the strap. As he finished and stood, her eyes, lit by the brilliant sun, were different, a deep fiery amber, and there were glints of dark red in her hair. He had to look away. He returned to the shelf of rock where he had left the cornet case, and he picked it up. Now he was ready. He waited for her to come to him, and then they made their way up the hill. At the top he took her hand to help her up the last steep rise.

They walked together through the park, and it was as if they were walking in the sky. They moved side by side, as if this was their marriage, in the sight of God and all the angels except the one who had first seen them, who had intended this, and he still hid his eyes. This was their marriage, this endless walk through the dappled green towards the white bandshell where he would take out the cornet and play "Carnival of Venice," alone, only for her. And the triple-tonguing would never be so perfect again, for he would soon abandon the cornet. He hadn't time for it, and for her, and for the study and pursuit of God. He would play for her, and then put the cornet away in the black case. He would play for her, standing tall and young in his best dark suit, as she stood below on the grass and drew the music from him, higher and brighter than ever before, his whole body roused and vivid, the sound of the cornet filling the park, the last high note slowly vanishing into the space of the sky.

Rose was working on the bird-cage when the bell rang. It was impossible to hear a knock when the power tools were on, so she'd rigged an electric bell on the back door. She glanced over her shoulder and saw the long bent figure of Curwan Brant at the foot of the outside steps. Since Curwan had retired from the ministry, he had nothing to do with his time, apart from a little hospital visiting, highly dangerous, Rose was sure, to all those on whom it was inflicted. She wondered if he'd dropped in merely to alleviate his boredom. The front door was locked at this hour. Perhaps Curwan was here wanting to get at the bishop. From time to time he came to see Henry with bizarre proposals – once he wanted to produce crossword puzzles based on the lives of the saints for use in Sunday schools. The bishop was surprisingly blunt with him, Rose always thought, when most would have been evasive or condescending.

"It wouldn't work, Curwan," he said of the crossword puzzle idea. "They don't know anything about the saints, and they don't care about the saints. But they're lovely little things all the same."

Rose knew that she could never speak to him so simply, so directly. If she had said those words, they would have been rude. There was something about the office of bishop, the sense of its significance, that led to freedom of speech. Or perhaps that was only an excuse. The bishop had a delicacy that Rose lacked. And even then, his response left Curwan irascible, full of sarcasm.

Rose pushed aside the pieces of the bird-cage; she didn't have the strength of mind to explain to anyone, and especially Curwan, that she was making an intricate wooden bird-cage although she didn't have or intend to have a bird to put in it. It had struck her one day when she had seen an old wire bird-cage in a pile of trash that the bird-cage was an interesting form, and she began making sketches of various kinds that could be made from wood. At first she planned to use commercial dowelling for the bars, but then she thought better of it and decided to turn the delicate spindles on her lathe. The problem was that she could only turn short lengths, otherwise they would break under the pressure of the chisel; so she'd been forced to redesign the cage so that she could make it with short lengths. She'd decided to make it from a variety of fruit-woods so that there was a matching of textures and colours.

The bell rang a second time. Rose opened the door of the workshop.

"Come in, Curwan."

He walked stiffly, like some great heron.

"I've never been in your workshop," he said.

He looked around him disapprovingly, as if he were about to drive the money changers from the temple, his head turning from side to side, the eyes bulging a little. On his tall legs, he looked like a crane; Rose remembered a story from Aesop in which a crane devoured a great number of frogs. She couldn't quite remember what the point of that story was. Curwan's larynx bobbed as a frog went down. Another.

"A great deal of machinery," he said.

"Yes."

"It must make a lot of noise."

"I work at night. The bishop doesn't mind the noise. No one else is here."

"Dust," he said.

"I clean it up."

"I have a chair," he said.

So that was the point of the visit.

"Broken," he said tragically.

"You want me to repair it?"

"I thought you might. It's a straight sort of chair. For sitting on, you know. At the table."

"Where is it?"

"In the car."

"Let's have a look."

They went up the steps and towards the car that was parked under a streetlight. It was an aged Plymouth, and there were holes rusted in the body. Not easy to buy a new car on a clergyman's pension, she supposed. Curwan opened the trunk and they stared down at the chair.

"Broken," Curwan repeated, "as you can see."

It was an unattractive oak chair, and two of the legs were snapped off where they joined the seat.

"Did you hit someone with it, Curwan? Or just throw it across the room?"

"Neither. As I'm sure you know."

"It's quite badly damaged."

"It was wobbly," he said. "I kept telling myself I ought to put a bit of string around it, but I put it off till tomorrow, and the next thing, there was Marjorie sitting on the floor and the chair as you see it."

"Was she hurt?"

"Not seriously," Curwan said. "Can you do anything?"

"I'm not sure it's worth it."

"It's one of a set."

Rose imagined a dim drawing room with a set of these fumed-oak chairs and matching fumed-oak table and Marjorie, who was a kind of fumed-oak colour, pouring tea in china cups. China cups with pink roses.

"I'll do what I can," Rose said.

"Will it be expensive?" Curwan said.

"I won't charge you anything except my materials. That won't be much."

"You are a true Christian, Rose."

Rose picked up the chair from the trunk of the car and carried it down to the workshop, Curwan following along behind. She found a place to put the wooden ruin out of her way in a corner, and turned back to Curwan, who stood on one foot in the middle of the room, swallowing frogs.

"Do you want tea?"

"That would be pleasant."

He followed her to the corner where she had the kettle and a small table and again he stood hunched.

"Sit down, Curwan," she said.

Rose assembled the materials for tea, going so far as to dig out a package of arrowroot biscuits.

"The bishop," Curwan said. "Is there any change?"

"No, not really."

Curwan had threatened a daily visit to pray over the mute body, but the dean had suggested the prayer might be as effectual from a distance. It seemed now as if Curwan might have decided to use her as his spy.

"He hasn't begun to speak?"

"He doesn't seem to care much whether he communicates, Curwan. He has the pad, but he seldom uses it."

"I see."

There was a long silence while Rose prepared the tea.

"His duties," Curwan said, getting to the point.

"Frank can handle a lot of it," Rose said. Frank was the bishop's assistant and director of programs for the diocese. He was pleasant and business-like – one of those excellent people, Rose thought, you can work with every day and still ignore. "And the dean and archdeacons can take on the ceremonial things."

"But it must leave a lot of loose ends."

Rose put the pot of tea on the table with two mugs, a plate of arrowroots and some milk in a cardboard container.

"If there are too many loose ends, presumably the archbishop will decide to do something about it."

Curwan brooded over the teapot.

"A committee," he said.

"What?"

"I thought we might form a committee. To help keep things in order while Henry's not himself. I have some free time these days, and I'd be pleased to help. I'm not without experience. And there are others like me. Old hands."

Rose poured the tea, and tried to imagine how she ought to respond to Curwan's proposal. What would the bishop have said? She could hear his voice, but no words that she could speak.

"I wouldn't think it was necessary," Rose said. "But you'd have to talk to Frank."

"I thought you might mention it."

"The bishop's secretary has no business trying to tell them how to run the diocese. And she would get slapped down if she tried."

"You have influence, Rose. It's known."

"Lots of things are known which aren't true."

"The bishop trusts you."

"That's true enough, but the bishop isn't making any decisions."

"He's always been a strange sort of man, unaccountable."

"The bishop?"

"Yes." He was pouring milk in his tea.

"I've always thought he was a kind, straightforward, saintly man."

"We're much of an age, Henry and I, though I'm a bit older. I knew him in college years ago. There were things. . ."

He sipped his tea.

"And there was the business with his wife." He left it hanging.

"His wife died a long time ago, didn't she?"

"Died. Well I suppose. Disappeared. Supposed dead. Well, strange things happen in the North. Months without contact with another white man. And before they went . . . But Henry's past that now. Saintly, was that how you put it? He's been popular. A popular bishop. And now just silence. Just lies there in silence. We must all pray for him."

Rose poured the hot tea into her mouth. She liked the way it scalded her tongue. It seemed to cleanse it. She didn't want to hear what Curwan was saying, didn't want to think about it. What he had said about the bishop repelled her. She drank her tea, would not speak. When Curwan came back for his chair, it would not be finished. She would let it sit, out of malice. She saw his Adam's apple bounce as he drank the tea, and she felt the panic of the frogs as they slipped down into that darkness.

Three floors above them, the bishop lay in his room, watched over by the night nurse; the thought calmed her. Perhaps Curwan was only laughable after all, with his crossword puzzle and his committee of old hands to help out. She was foolish to let the hint of old gossip touch her.

The pain in his shoulder was more intense now; he must convince himself that it was a form of beatitude. Perhaps the paralysis, the silence, was the discipline he needed; it would not allow him to be officious. Christians should not be merely busy with the Lord's work, skimming over the top of reality like a water strider. Now he was sodden, immersed in his body like one of the sunken punts in the river near his home when he was a boy. The boats with their flat bottoms and square sterns were docked at the edge of the slow brown water, and sometimes one would become waterlogged and sink into the mud. The owner might haul the boat out, dry it, caulk the joints, repaint it and try to set it afloat; or just as often it would be left to rot.

Henry was like that now, immersed. The darkness around him had a different texture for the fact that he could not shout across it, that he could move through it only with assistance. There were moments when he feared drowning, going down through the water, into the heavy wet mud, but he was an old boat now, the wood was soft and wouldn't take nails. It was time to let himself sink. To be still.

The pain in his shoulder flared. Sink down. He had a button to push for the nurse who would give him a pain-killer if he requested it, but he preferred to wait, to sink into the pain. God was in pain as much as he was in pleasure. He was there. God was what was there. He was. Is.

Think of the river, the small firm bodies of the bass he would pull from the water. The willows that hung over the water and were reflected in the rippled mirror.

The geography of that town where he had been a child and a young man was printed on the cells of his body; it was the well from which he drew all his understanding of life. The slow brown river with its grassy banks and patches of willows, the quiet street with picket fences, the cemetery behind the house that they could see from the back window, the boat dock where the river joined the lake, the park by the lake with its white bandstand (the echo of "Carnival of Venice" still ringing in the air as it rang in his inner ear, a memory of one kind of love), the high brick building that held the hardware store and above it his father's office, the church on its small hill, with the high maples that grew over it, the courthouse on the main street where his father had defended Percy Nash, when he was charged with murdering his brother, the yard behind the courthouse where Percy was hanged, the streets on the edge of town where the houses didn't have fences and dogs bred like wild animals, Amelia's house just on the borderline between that part of town and the part where he and his family lived, her mother desperate to grasp respectability so that she treated Henry as if he were royalty and embarrassed him by her attentiveness.

She was a worn woman with hair that had once been red but had grown thin and grey and strange yellow eyes. A nervous tic that afflicted the lid of one of the eyes and called attention to its odd colour. She was frightened of everything, and perhaps especially frightened of her dark daughter, who in her silence (and perhaps because her eyes and hair were those of the vanished father) was somehow imperious, though her words, few as they were, were polite. When Henry told the woman that he wished to marry Amelia, her face grew tight with panic.

"What about your family?"

"I've told them, and they approve."

His parents were kind to Amelia, invited her to sit with them in church, but probably they hoped that when he went away to school, he would lose interest; new things and new people would become part of his life. They believed that Amelia was wrong for him. Perhaps they were right, but it was impossible for Henry to think in those terms. There was no choice. He had been alone, and then she was a part of him. He no longer felt that he had to rehearse the words he said. Words came, as by an act of grace.

He was a boy sitting on the water, the old green punt

anchored in a shady spot, and then he was a young man sitting across the table from Amelia, who was laughing, and then he was alone again. He was a boy sitting in the old green punt with three bass in the slop of water that lay in the bottom, the big dead eyes staring at him, as God might stare if he were a God of malice, as the adversary might stare, accusing. Whenever he went fishing, he recalled that the disciples were fishermen, though they used nets as the commercial fishermen did still, out on the lake. He could see the nets drying on their big wooden reels. He tried to imagine Jesus coming and asking Fred Gordon and Bert Martin, as they leaned against their boats, smoking, to follow him and be his disciples. He couldn't imagine it somehow, and the failure troubled him, made him feel he didn't really understand Jesus after all.

The story of a life was the story of its errors. Even when he was a child, the stories about Jesus were never something that he could take for granted; he loved them too much, wanted to be close to them, part of them, and that always got things confused. He wanted to see Jesus call Fred Gordon and Bert Martin to follow him.

Henry remembered that boy's sublime innocent egotism, his desire to be part of the Bible story. It was the energy of a true commitment. His childish faith was wholly precipitate; wrong-headed or right-headed, the child hurled himself towards the mysteries of life and death.

Henry lay in the dark and tried to guess whether it was

time. His mother, when she had come to tuck him in, had drawn the maroon drapes across the window, and the room was so thick with darkness that all the daytime shapes, the wooden spindles at the end of his bed, his table, his chair, the box that held his toys, had vanished. Nothing in the room but the thick mysterious texture of darkness. Henry sat up and reached along the bed towards the foot. His covers fell off, and he was chilled, but he reached out until he could touch the spindles at the foot of the bed. The wooden spindles were still there. He could not see them, but he could touch them with his fingers. They were still there. It was like what his mother had told him about the dead: we cannot see them, but they are still with us. His grandmother was here near him, now, in the room, but in a different kind of darkness; he couldn't reach out and touch her the way he had touched the spindles.

On the wall across from his bed, he knew, though he could not see it, was "The Light of the World." Sometimes, as he lay in the blackness that was so close and still, Henry thought that the picture might begin to glow, that the Light of the World would shine out in his room, and it would be a miracle. It might happen when he was asleep and he would miss it, and he tried to keep himself awake to be ready, but he could never stay awake all night. His eyes would begin to shut, and he would pull himself awake and stare at the place on the wall where he thought the picture hung, all his mind concentrated, to help the Light materialize. The next thing it would be morning, and he would see sun shining under the door of his room and at the edges of the drapes, casting a pale red shadow back on the wall.

Henry remembered how he always fell asleep when he was waiting for the Light to come, and he was afraid if he lay back down now and covered himself, he would doze and wake in the morning when it was too late. The only safe thing was to dress now and go and wake Alice-Alice. He climbed carefully from the bed and, with his hands in front of him, began to move slowly across the room to the chest where he could find his clothes. If he opened the drapes, there might be moonlight to make it easier, but his mother or his father would hear and come and stop them.

His hands bumped the wall, and he slid them sideways until he found the edge of the chest. Henry was shivering hard now, and he didn't want to take off his night-dress and feel the cold on his skin. The house was making noises, small creaks and groans like those he'd heard his grandmother make when she had fallen asleep in her chair. His grandmother was here with him now. Like Jesus, but neither one made any noise. They were people, but they didn't make a sound; the house wasn't a person, yet it made noises in the night.

Henry pulled on his sweater over top of his night-dress; he knew his mother would disapprove, but he did it anyway. He was cold and confused in the dark. He had to crawl all over the room on his knees to find his shoes, and when he found them, he didn't put them on, just carried them in his hand. He put his other hand out in front of him and felt his way to the door. Sometimes the handle of the door squeaked when he opened it, and he hoped that this time it wouldn't. He thought of saying a prayer for it not to squeak, but he wasn't sure it was something he should pray about. Henry wasn't sure what God would think of the thing that he and Alice-Alice were planning, and since he wasn't sure, he thought it was safer not to pray that the handle didn't squeak. He turned it, and it didn't.

Once he was inside his sister's room, he tried to think how to wake her without giving her such a start that she would scream or cry out. He stood just inside the door of her room, and he could hear her soft breathing. It was a tiny, slow, comforting sound. Sometimes the breath grew so soft that he couldn't hear a thing. He remembered stories of how cats would steal a baby's breath to kill it, and this momentary kiss of air against air could so easily be lifted away and lost. Henry made his way on soft feet towards the bed, and he bent towards his sister's breathing as if he were the devil cat coming to kill her, but he only whispered her name softly.

"Alice-Alice. Alice-Alice."

He reached out his hand and put it on her. He could feel the warmth of her body, like bread his mother had taken from the oven. She made a little noise, like a word that couldn't find its way out of sleep and dreams.

"It's Henry," he whispered. "It's time."

"For what."

"You remember. Easter."

"I forgot. I was asleep."

"Don't say anything. Just get dressed."

Henry moved away from the bed to let Alice-Alice get out, and he felt his way back towards the door, to stand while she dressed. His shoes still held in his left hand, which was getting tired from holding them so tight, he listened to the soft thumpings and rustlings as his sister dressed herself. He liked being close to her in the dark like this, guessing what garments she was taking out and putting on.

"Henry?" The voice, whispering quietly in the darkness, was mysterious and unfamiliar, and for the first time, Henry was frightened at what they were doing. He went towards the place in the darkness that the whisper had come from, and they bumped together. He took hold of his sister's hand. They began to make their way along the hall towards the back stairs. At the top was another door to open, and then the steep curve to follow down to the kitchen, a door at the bottom too.

Then the kitchen, the shed, the garden.

Outside the air was colder, but there was a little light from the stars or from an invisible moon; it separated earth from sky and showed the larger shapes. Henry stopped to put on his shoes. They didn't have to walk as carefully, for the earth and the new grass were soft enough to cushion their steps. They crossed the lawn and the wide vegetable garden, unplanted, but freshly dug. Henry was shivering.

"Can we talk now?" Alice-Alice said.

"We better wait."

At the back of the vegetable garden, they found the

picket fence. Henry had climbed it before, but never in the dark. In the afternoon, he had put a wooden apple box beside it to help them over, but he was afraid someone might have noticed the box and moved it. His hands knocked against the pickets and then his toes struck the box.

"Here it is," he said, and he let go of Alice-Alice's hand and climbed on the box. It made it easier to get his leg over the fence, but his sweater caught on one of the pickets, and as he tried to get it off, his hand slipped and he fell on the other side of the fence. There was a shock as his body struck the earth, and then he was flat and paralysed, unable to breathe. He thought he was dying, for his breath would not come. If he was dying, he ought to pray, but he was too frightened to remember words.

"Henry?" his sister's voice was saying, "Henry? Talk. I'm frightened."

Henry noticed he was breathing again, and he sucked the air greedily.

"I fell," he said. "I couldn't breathe."

"I can't get over the fence."

Henry got up from the ground. At the fence he found his sister's hands, and he pulled as she struggled on the other side. As she came over the top, she almost tumbled, but Henry was able to stop her and help her down.

"Where are we going now?" Alice-Alice asked.

"We have to find someplace to wait."

"When will He come back?"

"Probably when the sun comes up."

"I don't want to go close to the graves."

"We want to be able to see."

"Are you sure He's going to come back?"

"Mother said that on Easter Jesus comes back from the dead. Mother doesn't lie."

"But I don't want to go near the graves."

"It's just all grass over them."

Henry had often stood at the back window and studied the graveyard that lay just beyond their back fence. Sometimes he'd seen someone bring flowers and stand with his head bowed, praying. On top, it was just all grass and stones with people's names, but underneath, he knew, the dead people lay.

"Will the other dead people come back?"

"Mother just said Jesus. But she said Granny was still here, but we can't see her."

"Maybe when Jesus comes back, you can't see him."

"Mother said he appeared to the disciples."

"Are we disciples?"

"I don't know. I'm not sure what one is."

"I'm cold."

"We have to find someplace to wait."

"Do we have to go close to the graves?"

"We'll just stay at the edge."

"All right."

When they stopped speaking, the silence and darkness of the night seemed to swell over them, and they stood still, afraid to move. At the other side of the cemetery, a small animal scuttled through the grass. There was a tiny voice of wind. Henry reached for his sister's hand and led her a little into the cemetery. There was a shape in front of him, one of the gravestones, and they sat down beside it. They sat close together for comfort against the cold and the night and the terrible, thrilling possibility that Jesus might appear.

"Maybe we should do something," Alice-Alice said.

"What?"

"Sing a hymn or say prayers."

Henry started to sing "Jesus Christ Is Risen Today," but his voice wasn't right and then he couldn't remember the words.

"Anyway, somebody might hear us," he said.

"So?"

"They'd make us go back to bed and we wouldn't see Jesus come back from the dead."

"Maybe he doesn't come back right here. There's other places with dead people."

"Maybe he comes to all of them."

"How?"

"I don't know."

They were silent again. Henry liked it better when they talked, but he couldn't think of anything to say. He and Alice-Alice sat very close together, and he was only warm where he touched against her. His eyes strained to penetrate the darkness, and he could see the repeated vertical shapes of the pale headstones. They were wavering in front of him, and something inside him was wavering as well, and his sister's breathing moved in and out with the same rhythm.

It was light, golden and airy, and he knew that someone was watching him. His eyes searched and discovered her where she stood a few feet away, her bare feet white and bony in the long stems of the grass. Each blade of grass had drops of water on it, and Henry felt wet, as if he too was covered with drops of water, and when he looked up at her face, he saw the water of tears coming from her dark eyes. Her fine dark hair hung loose, uncombed. Henry had only time to think that he didn't know who she was or why she was watching him or why she was crying, when his eyes closed, and then it was full daylight, and his father was waking them and carrying them back to the house.

Rose lay in bed and tried to think of something that she might make for the bishop, but he cared for nothing earthly now. The only thing he would have any use for was a coffin, but she couldn't very well start to manufacture one while he lay there alive, with every possibility that he might get better. Except he didn't want to get better, she suspected; not that he wanted to die — he seemed still full of life in a way — but he seemed to have taken the opportunity offered by the stroke to let loose all his attachments. She should knock together a good big pine box, carry it up to his apartment, and set him in it with a couple of pillows. Who was it slept in a coffin? Some saint? No, Sarah Bernhardt, who had no claim to sainthood that Rose had ever heard of.

Rose didn't want him to go. To leave her. When she thought of him lying there, not caring what went on around him, not caring that Rose needed his presence, his smile, she could grow quite irritable. Foolish, to be feeling like a betrayed lover just because the man had been afflicted with a cerebral haemorrhage. When she had found him, and realized what the trouble was, there had been a moment when she wanted to lie down beside him, or perhaps pick him up and carry him to the hospital in her arms, as if he were her child.

The thinkers all blabbed on as if the types of love were distinct, as if any fool could tell *eros* from *agape* and *agape* from *philia*, but Rose had never found it so simple. There was hot charity and cold, and, though she was no expert, she suspected that lust came in as many flavours as ice cream. She would not waste her life looking for a word for what she felt for the dear old man who lay imprisoned in silence, but she knew that the world would be emptier when he was not in it. She didn't want him to abandon her. If Rose had kept her distance from the world, it was perhaps because she had always feared loss, feared that she would always be finally abandoned.

Joanne. It was time Rose sent her a letter. The last time Rose had visited, she thought perhaps she preferred Paul, Joanne's husband, to the capable wife and mother who was her old friend. Yet there had been a time. A time when. A time when what? Rose had no words for that either; it was always a matter of such little things, moments, incidents that were there and then gone, the way Joanne would lift her fingers to her face as she listened to Rose talking to her. She had soft, tiny hands and pale golden hair. They'd met half-way through high school; they were both good students, and both a little outside things. Their paths ran together, and then apart. Joanne moved, somehow, into the centre of life, and Rose moved to the periphery, but for a while, they had shared a place on the edge, ironic observers and judges, satiric deflators of the adolescent world's follies and pretension. Joanne had begun going to church because Rose did, yet it was Joanne who got asked to join the choir and who became central to the church's existence, with her lovely voice and saintly air, the intense blue eyes in the small pale face. Perhaps only Rose knew that Joanne was sometimes laughing at those who treated her with such reverence. Rose was half-expected to be something less than perfectly pious because of the shape of her face and body. Joanne couldn't help it that she looked like a nun. Sometimes as they sat in church listening to the sermon, Rose would catch Joanne's eye and there would be a little flash of something, and afterward Rose would invent for Joanne a new story about Chicken Literal, the fundamentalist.

Once they were making brownies for a church tea, and Joanne suggested they add a package of Ex-Lax. They didn't quite dare, but when they were serving the brownies at the church tea, neither one could keep a straight face and they got sent home, and all the way along the street, they giggled as they invented tales of what might have happened if they'd actually done it.

When they got home, Rose's mother, listening to their laughter, asked the reason, and when she was told, disapproved and somehow blamed Rose for their naughty thought, though it had come from Joanne. It was always like that with Joanne. Could it be that there was some inevitable truth to physical appearance, innocence being some part of what Joanne was, even if it was something in her that she herself didn't understand or grasp? Rose thought sometimes that Joanne was a mirror and that her edge of cynicism was only the reflection of something in Rose, not something that was truly her own. She was a moon that shone with reflected light.

Rose puzzled over her in those days; she puzzled over it all. She had no words to understand it, but when she sat alone in her room at night, she would remember Joanne's face looking at her, and she would try to see it whole in her mind, but she could only remember individual features – the odd bareness when Joanne pulled back her hair, the curved line of her eyebrows, the soft down in front of her ear, the blue, slightly protruberant eyes. She would feel the eyes looking at her, always observing, silent, unreachable somehow.

Well, it was different now, and simpler. She would write a letter. Rose drew her thoughts away from the past. She brought the image of the bird-cage into her mind, turning it round to see it from all sides. It was, she was afraid, too symmetrical, as if it ought to have some inner divisions to make it more than a mere cube; but would inner divisions make any sense? If they were done right.

She could make small panels, with bevelled edges, so that the cage had a variety of inner forms, depending on where the panels were inserted. Rose switched on the light beside the bed and climbed out; her drafting board was at the other side of the room, and she went to it and stood there in her pyjamas, sketching out possibilities for these sliding panels. It was a complicated problem to create them without adding too much framework and making the cage heavy. Part of its appeal was the lightness, the sense that it was as much a part of the air as the bird. As she finished one of the sketches, she found herself sketching the form of a bird inside. Ridiculous; she didn't want a bird, all that gravel, bird droppings and seed spread around the floor, the insistent duty of providing it food or water, the fear that it would sicken and die for some inexplicable reason. This was not the cage for a real bird, but for some perfected spiritual bird.

Of course.

She would carve a bird, out of something soft, pine or cedar, carve it and perhaps paint it with colours that no bird had ever had, or in the colours of some lovely bird that she could never have caged, a cardinal or a pine grosbeak, or some kind of woodland sparrow. She'd have to consult some reference books. And once she had finished it, she would take it to the bishop to make up to herself for the Bible box that was rushed and imperfect. She would hang the cage where he could see it from his bed, the hardwoods waxed and shining, the bright eye of the wooden bird watching over him like a guardian spirit.

Norman curled tight in his corner and tried to keep his eyes shut. Night was worst because of the Dark Angels. At night the Angels went away and the Dark Angels came, but Thy Spirit could come anytime. He lay in the darkness, trying not to open his eyes. He reached out and touched the soft feathers of the messenger pigeon, and that made him feel better. He tried to think about good things. He thought about Patrick. Patrick was always good to him, better than anyone else. They met one afternoon when Norman was at the stadium staring through the fence at the Hell Drivers, watching them put up the barriers and ramps. Some of the drivers were working on their cars, and Patrick had grease on his hands and arms when he came over to the fence. He asked Norman if he wanted a job, and when Norman said sure, he brought him inside the gate and told Al that Norman would help him carry some of the barriers. Al fooled around a lot while they were doing it, and made Norman laugh, and after a while Al went over to Patrick and talked for a while and then they said did Norman want to be part of the show that night. Norman told them he didn't know how to drive a car, but they said he didn't have to, that he'd be a clown with Al. Norman was scared that he wouldn't know how, but they said he just had to follow Al and do everything he did.

Patrick gave him some money to buy a hotdog, and then Al took him to a room underneath the grandstand to get him ready. Al had a big suitcase with the clown suits in it, and he got out one for Norman and one for himself. The only time Al got mad was when they were starting to go out, and he saw Norman's buttons weren't done up.

When they had the suits on, and the paint on their faces, they sat on the bench in the little room and stared at the walls until it was time to go out. Then, they went through a cement hallway and a little door. Outside the door, it was night, but there was bright light shining on the cars. Norman heard noises from up above, but when he turned around to look, the lights shone in his eyes and he couldn't see. Then he noticed people in the seats, and one of them waved.

Al got some things out of a trunk, big shoes and a big soft thing like a baseball bat. He told Norman how to turn around and Al would hit him on the ass with the bat and Norman would fall down, and he showed him how to put two balloons in his clown suit and pretend they were big tits and walk like a girl, and then fall down and break them.

The cars were starting, the noise of the engines so loud that Norman couldn't hear what Al was saying to him any more. The drivers were running out to their cars, and he heard the crowd cheering over the sound of engines, then the big revving. Norman was laughing at it all, then Al started to laugh and they went out into the lights to do the act. They ran and fell down and waved and everything Al did, Norman imitated as closely as he could. They put the balloons in their shirts and Norman walked like a girl then fell down and one of his tits didn't break so he went down again and this time it did. Al hit him with the bat and Norman fell down again.

Then Al ran out in front of where the cars were coming and waved his arms to stop a car, and when the car stopped Al went and shook hands with the driver, and Al and Norman got on the front of his car, and he drove them over to their bench.

They went out once more before the show was over, then Patrick flew his car over a bunch of other cars, and then it was the end. Before they went inside, some little kids came to talk to Al and Norman, and once Norman got talking to them, he couldn't stop, even after the kids went and they were back in the little room. No matter how hard he tried, he couldn't keep himself from talking, and Al started to laugh and said Norman was stage-struck. Norman didn't know what it was, but he talked about that too while they took off their clown suits and their makeup. Norman kept talking even when Al told him to try and be quiet; he'd remember something that happened when they were out there under the lights, and he'd have to talk about it. He knew he was making Al laugh at him, but he couldn't stop.

When Patrick came into the room, Norman found himself telling him the same things. That was when Patrick and Al went into the corner of the room and then came back and asked Norman if he wanted to have a job with them. He would travel with them and be a clown with Al.

Norman went with them and got to be good at all the tricks, his tits always broke the first time he fell, and he'd stagger and make a dive when Al hit him with the bat.

That was good to think about, and so was when he was first with Glory, and the'd get some beer and some Kentucky Fried Chicken and how they'd laugh. Glory would give little bits of chicken to the white cat, and they'd laugh at how she cleaned herself after she ate it.

The best part with the Hell Drivers was the clown makeup. The first time, he didn't know what Al was doing when he told Norman to sit down in front of him and took some cold white stuff and rubbed it all over Norman's face. He took out some fat crayons, a white one and a red one and a black one, and started to draw on Norman's face. He told Norman to close his eyes, and Norman felt Al's fingers rubbing the stuff on his face. Then he opened his eyes, and Al drew around his mouth with the red crayon and then on his cheeks and then lines around his eyes with the black crayon. He had a little red ball in his suitcase and he put it over Norman's nose with some elastics around his head. Then he pulled out some orange hair, and he put it on Norman's head; it was tight, and it squeezed behind his ears and almost hurt.

Al made more marks with the white crayon, and then he held out a mirror. Norman saw a face with a big red smile and funny eyes and a red nose and orange hair. He couldn't believe it was his own face.

Norman opened his eyes. He could see the little light at the end of the Pipe Hole, but there was nothing coming. He listened, but there was no sound. He didn't know what the Dark Angels would sound like, but he was sure that when he heard them, he would know what it was.

Henry could not see them, and yet he knew that they were somewhere near. As he drifted across the grass of the field, the mist swayed like a pale fabric from the movement of the others behind it. They never came into sight, and he knew that he mustn't shout, that calling out to them would be wrong, but it was a comfort to know that they were there, all of them, his father and mother and Alice-Alice and Amelia. They were on their way to some important event; perhaps it was his wedding.

Behind the curtains of mist, the green of grass and leaves was half-visible, a green fire lost in its smoke. His footsteps led him across the field to the water. That was where they would meet, and where the ceremony would be held. He was impatient to be married to Amelia, and as he walked, he reached out his arms into the fog, and he was sure that in a moment his fingers would find her, and he would hold her against his chest.

He could hear the sound of the water, and he tried to walk faster, but now there was a hill, and he could only ascend it with slow care. The grass was heavy with water; it was hard to move his feet through it.

Then he was at the top of the hill, and through the mist he could see them gathered below him. He made his way down, but each time he looked, the figures in the pale mist had moved, and he began to wonder if they were not the loved ones he had thought to meet. Perhaps these were strangers, and he stared into the fog, looking for the features of his father or his mother.

He did not dare to look for Amelia.

He knew that all these people who were to meet him here had been dead, but now they weren't, they were here, yet he couldn't quite see them, couldn't quite touch them. His father would be the easiest to find; he was the most substantial, and if Henry could shake his hand, that warm grip would draw him through the curtain of pallor and let him be with the others.

Henry was shouting as he tried to explain that the wedding couldn't be held if these guests wouldn't come forward and join him. Amelia was too shy to be the first, he told them, they must precede her and show that it was safe, the wedding would truly happen, and then perhaps she would come to join them. Henry sat down on the edge of a log and he could see figures in the pews looking towards him and one coming up the aisle in a white dress. She knelt before him to be confirmed, and he put his hands on her in blessing, but she kept her face averted so that he couldn't see her features, and Henry wouldn't say the words of confirmation until she looked at him. He could tell that people in the pews were beginning to whisper and point towards them, and he was gripping her harder and harder with his hands. The congregation began to sing, and Henry rose from the bishop's throne and made a slow recessional walk towards the cathedral door.

Outside, he was in a familiar street of small brick houses, each one with a title embossed in Hebrew letters; no matter how Henry puzzled over the letters, he could make nothing of them. There was a kosher poultry shop with golden letters on the window, and behind the window, chickens flew up and down, feathers falling from them as they flew, and the cloud of feathers was like the mist. Through the whirling plumage, he could see a dark figure; this was the *shochet*, the ritual slaughterer who was chasing the chickens and making them fly wildly about the room. Henry could see nothing of the figure except a shadow, until suddenly a bearded face stared out the window, a bearded face in a black hat, and wearing a white shirt. The face observed as Henry walked by, past another row of houses until he came to the one he sought.

He was in the kitchen where Jacob's father was staring across the table towards him. The old man picked up a glass of tea from in front of him and sipped it. Then he raised his hand and shook it at Henry for emphasis as he spoke.

"Listen, Henry. Rabbi Johanon ben Zakai said: 'If you should have a sapling in your hand when they tell you that the Messiah has arrived, first plant the sapling and then go to greet the Messiah.' "

There was a silence as he bent to sip his tea.

"Do you understand that, Henry?" he said gently. "Now that you're old, do you understand what Rabbi Johanon ben Zakai was trying to teach?"

"I don't have a sapling in my hand," Henry said.

"Childish," the man said. "Don't be childish, Henry."

Embarrassed by his own foolishness, Henry left the house, and now when he walked down the street, the poultry store was gone, and he was once again searching for a way to the beach where he would meet Amelia, and they would be married.

Awake, Henry lay in the dark, and the images of the dream seemed to hang in the air, as if they had been painted there and presented to him for inspection. Considering them, he felt too naked; the filters that made memory safe had been taken from him, and the past came upon him with all the vividness of the moment before a car accident, when the shock of adrenalin saturating the brain makes reality slow and huge. What was the source of this symptom now? Was it some chemical created by the stroke or by the brain's attempt to heal? Was it the result of his lying here, some chemical derangement of the apparatus?

He put the thought aside. Henry cared less for such explanations than for the phenomenon itself, the closeness of these men and women from his past. If he had another lifetime ahead of him, he would have devoted it to the exploration of memory and ghosts, all the kinds of presences that secretly touched the mind and body.

They had been so near to him in the dream, and yet he had neither seen nor touched them; they had only been shadows that came towards him and then vanished. Even the candidate for confirmation would not show him her face, though he knew from the shape of her head, her bent shoulders, who she must be.

Jacob's father had been clear – the balding head, the quick eyes, the large, somehow oddly expressive, broad nose. And the words, it seemed to Henry, were words that Samuel Goldberg had actually spoken to him, one of the many challenges he threw out to him, like any teacher of the spirit who presents mysterious remarks and leaves his disciple to make sense of them.

Henry had met Jacob, the wise old man's first son, at Hart House one day, when he had gone there for the mid-day prayer service and then discovered that the service was being taken by a Presbyterian minister whose Calvinist attitudes always troubled him. Henry had turned away from the chapel and hurried into one of the nearby common rooms where he stood at the window, staring across the snowy campus and examining his conscience in the matter. Did he merely hold it against the man that he was of a different Protestant denomination? Did his personal preference justify skipping the service or was it just a kind of self-indulgence, spiritual laziness? He thought perhaps it was, and yet, it had always seemed to Henry that anything at all that turned his mind from God was a hindrance to his faith, even if the thing that turned his mind called itself by a holy name.

The young man stood at the window for a long time as he struggled with his feelings and beliefs. He was so serious, so earnest and determined to try too hard; as Henry remembered him, he wondered, momentarily, if his own refusal to torment his conscience was a spiritual tiredness as much as it was wisdom. Perhaps, but it was also what he had learned from Samuel Goldberg; not to urge his faith towards false intensities. First plant the sapling and then go to greet the Messiah.

The young Henry turned from the window of that

Hart House common room, as if to make a decision, but then stood still, hesitant. He could not make up his mind. The room was empty except for a good-looking young man who sat on a couch nearby with a magazine. Henry found himself staring at the man. Their eyes met.

"You look worried," the man said.

Without hesitation, Henry went and sat down beside him and told him all of what was going through his mind. He half expected to be laughed at, but Jacob took him seriously, and though he explained that as a Jew he didn't perfectly understand the distinctions of the various kinds of Protestant worship, still anyone who had been brought up by his father must have a great, even a grave, appreciation of the subtleties of theological speculation and the related pangs of conscience.

"I've never talked to a Jew before," Henry said. He thought perhaps he was being rude, but his words were moving ahead of his mind.

"Do you want to convert me?"

"I don't know. I don't know anything about you."

They talked for an hour, and Henry was startled to find in Jacob a kind of seriousness that was new to him. He wasn't, like Henry's friends in theology, pious; in fact he wanted to move away from his father's obsession with religion, and yet he had an unembarrassed ability to discuss ideas and intellectual passions.

"You must meet my father," he said to Henry as they left Hart House, turning in opposite directions towards their afternoon classes, and later, after a couple of meetings with Jacob that were not altogether chance, Henry did meet the man, and even developed the habit of dropping in at the Goldberg house to visit. The first time, he was treated a bit formally, but soon Samuel Goldberg began to talk to him about Judaism, to drop bits of the Talmud in front of him, as if to see if he would pick them up or merely step around them. Samuel would dip his moustache into a glass of tea, drink, lift his head and suck the tea from the hairs and stare at Henry, who might be licking from his lips the last taste of poppyseed cake.

"Rabbi Tarphon," Samuel Goldberg would say, and pause to make sure that he had Henry's attention, "Rabbi Tarphon says 'You are not required to complete the work, but neither are you free to desist from it.' "

Henry would nod and let the saying ring in his mind like a phrase of music. When he got back to his room, he would write it down; he had the feeling that it would be many years before he understood what was at issue in his conversations with this man. Yet he came back, again and again, to ask questions, to listen. He had never, even at the theological college, met anyone who talked with such ease about God. While Henry and Samuel talked, Jacob would sit by in silence, or simply go away, into another room. He was a man of the secular world. He wanted to succeed, and he would assimilate without anxiety in order to do it.

Once Henry dared to bring up the question of Jesus, his role as the Messiah, the Son of God.

"The Messiah," Samuel said, "is where he belongs, in

the beauty and safety of the future. Like Israel. 'Next year in Jerusalem,' we say, but inside we know it must *always* be next year. The Zionists are wrong."

Henry knew little of Zionism until Samuel explained it to him that day, an explanation from the lips of a man who opposed and feared it. Henry had lost touch with the Goldbergs after he left university, but he had often wondered if Samuel's dislike of Zionism had been altered by the events in Germany.

Perhaps in the dream he should have asked that question, as if the dream were real. If a dream were treated as real, did it become so? What is real is what we give ourselves to. He had thought sometimes that a just God might allot each person, in an afterlife, the thing they had expected; to believe a doctrine, a dream, a vision of hell, a vision of heaven, was to cause it to become true. This was a doctrine that would have appealed to Samuel Goldberg, something fluid and ironic. He hated doctrinal rigidities.

In the days and nights after each visit, Henry found himself confronting the core of Christian doctrine with the devout irony that he discovered from Samuel, and he began to fear that the old man might be dangerous. Henry had known nothing about Jews except that they were treated with fear and contempt. In his uneasiness, Henry tried to tell Curwan Brant about his visits. Curwan was a little older than Henry, and was about to graduate from his theology course. He was active in the campus YMCA, and on the student executive of the theological college. He had taken an avuncular interest in Henry from the time they had met, though Henry found Curwan's Christianity a bit too warlike. He knew, before he spoke, that Curwan would disapprove of the Goldbergs, but he felt that he couldn't keep them a secret. If he was ashamed to talk about Samuel Goldberg, he shouldn't see him.

Curwan disapproved, as Henry knew he would.

"We can't have anything to do with a race that denies the divinity of Christ, Henry. You know what they said. *'His death be upon us and upon our children.'* What we can do is pray for their conversion."

"But Samuel Goldberg is a man who loves God."

"Do you remember what Paul said? 'Brethren, my heart's desire and prayer to God for Israel is, that they might be saved. For I bear them record that they have a zeal of God, but not according to knowledge.' *Not according to knowledge,* Henry."

"Do you think they're going to lead me astray, Curwan? If so, you don't have much trust in my Christian faith."

Curwan looked intensely at him.

"I'll pray for you, Henry. And I'll pray for them."

It was late winter the day Henry met Jacob, and all through the weeks of spring, he let himself be drawn to the Goldberg's house to listen to Samuel. He was disturbed sometimes that he himself didn't do more talking, didn't make any attempt to bring the Goldbergs to Christ, as Curwan and his teachers would have demanded of him. Henry excused himself with the explanation that he was too young, only a student, still learning. He had no business trying to convert a sophisticated Jew until he was older.

Now in the silence of his final room, he wondered what, if he met Samuel Goldberg now, he would have to say to him. Would he, a bishop, a man as learned in Christianity as he would ever be, have the courage to try to convert him? No. If he met Samuel now, he would only be able to thank him for his kindness to that young man, for the wisdom he had offered.

And even now, all these years later, Curwan would have hated such tolerance. His first thought still, faced with a Jew, would be to seek his conversion. Yet it was Henry who had become a bishop. Was it only the consequence of his diplomatic and administrative skills, or was his voice, in some way, the true voice of the church? Whatever Henry was, Samuel Goldberg had helped to form him.

He had tried to teach Henry not to question his conscience too strenuously. He told him about Rabbi Israel Baal-Shem Tov, how he taught that men should be rid of their sadness.

"Even if a man has committed a sin," Samuel exclaimed, "he shouldn't be too sad. Or maybe he'll neglect the service of God. He should be sad because of the sin, yes, of course, but he should return to rejoice in the Creator, praised be He."

The room where they sat was warm, crowded. On the table were Mrs Goldberg's poppyseed cakes. Samuel's eyes, heavy, wet, seemed almost to caress him as the older man repeated the beloved words.

"He should be sad because of the sin, but he should return to rejoice in the Creator, praised be He."

Samuel drank from his glass.

"Do you understand, Henry?" he asked.

"Yes," Henry said. "I do."

Late that night, Henry walked the streets back to the university. He could smell the new leaves, the freshness of spring in the air. Everything was still, contained, perfected, as if, at that moment, it was seen only by the eye of God. The moment was something achieved, a possibility that had come to fruition. Time was forgiven.

Soon after that night, the end of term arrived, and Henry went home for the summer. When he returned in the fall, he couldn't often find a free evening to go to the Goldbergs. Through the rest of his time at university, his visits were occasional, and they were without the intensity of that first winter and spring, but he always felt that Samuel Goldberg remained a part of him, a voice that would catch him by surprise now and then, when a thought that seemed at first foreign to him would lodge in his being, and gradually, as he pondered it, he would hear it expressed in Samuel's voice. His one great lesson was not to make God too unusual. Jesus, crucified, was such a dramatic figure; the world was a battle of good and evil. What Samuel had tried to give him was the realization of God as a simple part of day-to-day life. That was the point of the Torah, of *kashruth*. God was on the table with the evening meal. Henry had always treasured the story of the Roman Pompey, who, when he had conquered Jerusalem, profaned the Holy of Holies, the most sacred part of the temple where even the High Priest was only allowed on the Day of Atonement. Pompey broke in to know what was there, to answer the gossips' question. What was so secret that no man could observe it? And there was, of course, nothing to be seen. If one could disregard the blood that Pompey spilled to make his way there, it was a wonderful joke played by Jehovah on one of the foolish *goyim* who could understand nothing but idols, sculpture, buildings, the insignia of the legions, the piling up of goods in the triumph through the streets of Rome.

They conquered Jerusalem and carried its treasure to Rome. First the legionaries, then the apostles. It was one of the great mysteries, the passion that existed between the church and Rome. The instrument of martyrdom became the instrument of salvation as the city of man and the city of God, which were two, became both two and one, like a double exposure. Or in another double exposure, Rome and Jerusalem became both of them the earthly symbol for the city of God. The Book of Acts was in ways the most fascinating and mysterious book in the Bible as it traced in its hesitant, desultory way, the separation of Christianity from Judaism, the movement from Jerusalem to Rome, from the High Priest in his Temple to the Bishop in his cathedral.

When he was still able to move – still *alive* he found himself phrasing it – Henry had liked to stand at the front window and contemplate the shape of this, his last cathedral. Some years before, he had stood on its porch, vested in his robes and mitre, about to enter for his installation as bishop of this diocese; as part of the ancient ceremony, he must stand at the cathedral door and knock for admission. Inside they were waiting for him, the faithful of the diocese and their officers, the cathedral clergy, the choir. The organ was prepared to play him welcome. Dilatory, unready, Henry stood on the porch, though it was a cold December evening and a few flakes of snow were falling in the night air, hints of what would come later that night, the first real fall of snow. The archdeacons shivered and paced impatiently, but Henry couldn't quite bring himself to knock with his crozier and enter into his role here.

He had no family there with him at his installation. Alice-Alice had written from New Zealand and said she would be praying for him. Henry thought of her praying quietly to herself on the other side of the globe. He looked around him and studied the flakes of snow.

He must stop dawdling; the children would be growing impatient. In the absence of a family, Henry had brought a gang of local children that he had picked up from the streets. He had spent a morning walking near the cathedral, finding children and asking them if they would be his family for the service of installation. One or two ran away in fright, but most agreed to take Henry to their parents and make the arrangements.

"I have no children of my own," he would say to each

mother, and usually they accepted this as sufficient explanation for his somewhat bizarre request. Now, inside the cathedral, seated near the chancel, was his little group, in the place his family would have held. Years before, when he was first made a bishop, he had listened to the words of the epistle pass over him, the demand that he be "the husband of one wife . . . one that ruleth well his own house, having his children in subjection with all gravity," and his possible, impossible children rose up before him in rebellion, but they were unseen, unheard.

A week before the wedding. He and Amelia were in the parlour of his parents' house. She was standing in front of the piano, her small fingers caressing the keys. She didn't know how to play, but she seemed fascinated by the instrument, as if it held some kind of magic; Henry suggested that later she might take lessons, but she insisted she couldn't learn. Yet she couldn't help putting her fingers on the instrument, as she was now. He had walked into the room, and he was startled, once again, by her beauty, by the fact that they would marry, that she would be his to cherish. The light from the window caught her face as it turned towards him, her lips a little open, one of her ears and the one side of her face shining softly. Their eyes met, and Henry was so touched by something in her look that he wanted to lift her up and carry her through water and fire. Their life lay ahead of them, sunlit, brilliant, infinitely desirable.

He tried to tell her what he was feeling; he talked about the wonder of their future, the blessedness of their sharing, but when he mentioned having children, her face changed, and something in it became distant. The words he was speaking went dead in his mouth. He remembered what he had felt the day before, when they had walked along the street together. It had rained in the night, and Henry noticed earthworms on the pavement, stranded and lost on the baked concrete in the bright sun. Each time he saw one, he lifted it and put it on the grass or earth nearby. After he had done it several times, Amelia, who had watched him in silence, spoke.

"They're going to die anyway. They're half dead now."

"Some of them might live," he said. "One or two. We're not in a hurry anyway, are we?"

He smiled at her, but something in him was broken.

The snow fell faster as Henry, standing by the door, prepared himself for his new place as overseer of the spiritual life of this new flock. His temporary family awaited him. Passing along the street at the edge of the porch were two young boys. They stopped and stared, and Henry was inclined to ask if they wanted to join his children inside.

"Who's he?" one of the boys said.

"Can't you tell?" the other one shouted. "It's Santa Claus."

"Are you Santa Claus?" the first one yelled to him.

"No," Henry said.

"I'll bet he's one of the wise men. Are you?"

"Well," Henry said, "I hope so."

He turned and knocked his crozier on the wooden door.

Rose steered her bicycle along the edge of the road by the lake. The water was serenely flat in the windless morning, and the sunlight lay over it, a sheen of vividness. Rose had wakened early and what she had wanted was to ride immediately to the old house where the bishop lay, to reassure herself, to know, that he was still in the world, but she had restrained herself, and as she lay there, she tried to pray for him, but everything was too far away. She wondered sometimes if her faith was not in God, but only in the human beings who seemed to speak to her for God — the bishop here, one or two people at the mission where she'd worked in Toronto. It was necessary to find God in despair, but was it possible to find him in simple human loneliness? Didn't you need the reassurance of human contact?

The bishop had travelled alone for so many years. Rose imagined him as a clergyman, still young, arriving in a new parish, among strangers, standing in the sanctuary looking out over the unknown faces, some of them only too eager to search out his weaknesses, with nothing for company but the familiar words of the prayer book, and the presence of what he worshipped. It was a lot to bear. Rose needed the presence of friends to provide a home for her faith. Even Christ had chosen disciples. Paul had travelled with companions. It wasn't surprising that several of the Roman Catholic priests she'd met seemed to have something missing. It wasn't celibacy, but what too often accompanied celibacy, the lack of intimate human contacts. It was all very well to have God for your friend, but there must be, for most believers, those periods when God withdrew, when he maintained some distance; without friends, the cold was too great.

You knew, about Henry, without needing to be told, that he had married, that he understood intimacy and love, and if he had chosen not to marry a second time, it was out of the still-echoing intensity of the first, not because he wished to be without close human contact. When he laid his hands on a candidate for confirmation, his touch was always passionate and gentle.

Rose turned the corner and began to peddle up the street that led to the diocesan offices and the bishop's apartment. Beside her were the green lawns of the cathedral, and the massive stone building sat in splendid silence. Somewhere inside, Chappie, the sexton, was running his vacuum cleaner, while the curate was preparing for the early communion.

There was someone sitting on the steps of the diocesan centre. He had dark skin and straight black hair with grey patches. When she pulled up her bike beside the steps, he turned and smiled at her. Under the thin hairs of the moustache, his teeth were ground down to brown stumps and a couple were missing, but the smile was wide and friendly. It reminded her for a moment of Henry's lovely smile.

"Hello," Rose said.

The man was wearing a heavy plaid shirt, unbuttoned, and under it was a T-shirt with a picture of Mick Jagger. There was a bag on the step beside him.

"Can I help you?" Rose said. She felt foolish.

"I came to see Henry."

"The bishop isn't very well."

"Yeah. He's dyin'."

The small figure remained on the steps, waiting for her to speak or make the next move. She expected him to start asking unanswerable riddles. His skin was weathered and deeply wrinkled, the face broad, with padded cheekbones.

"I'm Rose," she said.

"You could call me Joe."

"Is that your name?"

"No."

"Then why would I call you that."

"That's what most white men call me. It's my government name."

"What's your real name?"

"Ishakak."

"I'll call you that."

"OK."

Rose tried to puzzle out what to say next.

"How'd you cut off your finger?" the man asked.

"On a power saw. It was a long time ago."

"I cut off my toe once. Got frozen."

"Does that make it hard to walk?"

"Not bad."

"You must have known Henry when he was in the Arctic."

"I guess so."

"How did you know he was sick?"

"My helper told me."

"Your helper?"

"Mostly he's a bird. But sometimes a seal."

Rose was startled, confused, then put it together. He was a shaman.

"Did you come to help Henry get better?"

"No."

"Why not."

"You can't fix somebody when they want to die."

The old man's bluntness shocked her. Soon she was going to have to let him in the house or send him away. She studied the wrinkled face that seemed both energetic and impassive. His deep brown eyes had a kind of light in them that might be mischief.

"Do you still live in the North?"

"Yeah."

"How did you get down here?"

"Got a plane ride."

"You mean you bought a ticket?"

"No. Guy from Northern Affairs gave me a free ride."

"Why did he do that?"

"He asked me to put a spell on a girl he wanted to get."

"Did you?"

"Didn't have to. I already knew she wanted to do it.

After he got her, he says he'd do me a favour some time."

"So you came all the way down here to see Henry?"

"I guess so."

"Have you ever been up in a plane before?'

"No."

"It must have been exciting."

"I went to the moon a couple of times."

She stared into the bright eyes and tried to make out if he was joking with her. Perhaps he was a bit mad. She must decide what to do with him. The solution, she supposed, was to leave it up to the bishop. She would take the old man up to the bishop's bed and ask if he wanted him there or sent away.

"Do you want to come in and see the bishop, Ishakak?"

"That's why I came."

Rose went up the steps and unlocked the door, and Ishakak followed her. He was carrying a blue club bag with a strange insignia in yellow and red; it took her a moment to realize that it was the CBC logo, and when she worked that out, she couldn't help wondering where he'd picked it up.

As usual, Rose was the first to arrive at work, and the offices on the lower floors were empty. Rose led the way up the stairs. When they reached the apartment, the night nurse came to meet them. She was about to speak to Rose when she noticed the old man behind her.

"This is an old friend of the bishop's, from the Arctic," Rose said. "He's come to see him."

The nurse stared.

"I'll stay here till the day nurse comes," Rose said. "You can leave whenever you like."

"Yes. All right. He seemed to have a quiet night."

She picked up a white shoulder bag and marched down the stairs. Ishakak watched her go.

"Nice and fat," he said. "Keep him warm at night."

Rose pointed to the couch.

"She sleeps here," she said. She couldn't quite make out the tone of some of the man's comments, whether they were meant to be jokes or not.

"Doesn't smell too good, anyway. Maybe make him feel worse."

Rose couldn't help smiling. It was true. The night nurse wore an unpleasant perfume of some sort. The old man was smiling back at her.

"Come and see Henry," she said.

The bishop had heard them, and his head was turned towards them as they entered the room. He glanced at Rose, and then his eyes moved to meet those of the old Inuit. There was complete stillness in the room as the two looked at each other. Rose felt sure that the bishop was about to speak, as if the intensity of that long look must create new circuits in the brain to replace the damaged ones. The silent confrontation of the two men went on for so long that Rose began to feel that she must break it off, and yet she was the outsider now. It was something beyond her.

At last Ishakak began to talk, long flat consonantal

phrases, with a kind of clicking rhythm in them. After he had spoken for a long time, he sat down in the chair by the bed and began to open his bag. The bishop lay with his eyes closed. Rose watched the features of his face which went through a kind of struggle and then came to rest. She was free to speak.

"Bishop," she asked, "do you want Ishakak to stay with you for a while? He seems to be planning to."

The bishop's eyes met hers, and she thought for a moment that they might be wet with tears, but then they changed again, and he picked up the pencil that lay at his side.

"Do you want him left here with you?" Rose asked.

The hand slowly printed three letters. Yes.

In the meantime, the shaman had taken a piece of rope out of his bag. It had some bits of fur attached to it and strips of coloured cloth. He tied it around his waist. Rose turned and left the room. If the old man began doing magic, and word of it got out, it would lead to no end of fuss in the diocese. A few years ago, a church group had begun practising some form of witchcraft and faith healing and it had been a major scandal.

What was between these two men who now faced each other at the top of the house? It was many years since Henry had left the Arctic, and it was something that he didn't often talk about, at least in Rose's presence. There was no doubt that he had understood what Ishakak had said to him; he hadn't forgotten Inuktitut.

While she waited for Frank and the others to arrive,

Rose went to her office and began answering some of the easier letters, invitations from people who didn't know the bishop was ill, letters with best wishes from around the diocese. She didn't read him all the letters, but she gave him a list of those who had written, and a few of the more interesting ones she set up on the stand beside his bed where he could read them. There was a lovely note from Annie Huberland who said she'd been attending the cathedral for eighty years and he was her favourite bishop.

In a moment's pause in the clattering of her typewriter, she heard singing coming from the upper part of the house.

A voice intoned a repetitive drone with only two or three notes. As it went on and on, it made her nervous. She couldn't sit and work with that going on above her.

She climbed the stairs again, unable to think what she might do when she got to the top. What was happening seemed wrong, and yet to send the man away seemed wrong too. Rose disliked such moments, when the opacity, the total foreignness of human life, the incomprehensibility of it, faced her like a malicious dwarf. It was suddenly clear to her why so many people tried to reduce life to a formula, to make behaviour and speech a conventional ritual which provided at least the illusion that it was all explicable. How to explain anything when she found herself faced with this craziness, some doited old shaman appearing with a wild story and singing songs over Henry's paralyzed body? Paul's Letter to the Aphasians, Chapter 2,

Verse 2: *Let not the doctors of the pagan sing their songs over your flesh.*

Rose looked in from the doorway of the room. The old man had taken off his plaid shirt, and in a T-shirt, his compact body looked thick and powerful. He rocked slowly as he sang, as if he were in some kind of trance. On the table in front of him were two or three animal teeth, some feathers, and a pile of dark brown tobacco. Behind these was a human skull. One saw, on Halloween, dozens of stylized representations of such a thing, but this was no playful symbol. This was the head of a human being, and the holes where the eyes and nose had been were unseemly; it was something that should not be looked at. The jawbone was gone; the row of upper teeth was without gaps or breaks. It must be the skull of a young person. The shaman's song went on, as Rose stared at this piece of a corpse, and she felt herself suddenly implicated in something that was beyond her depth. She looked towards the bed where the bishop lay, his eyes closed, his face apparently at peace. Her eyes turned back to the skull, those shining teeth. There was something odd about them, something unbalanced.

On the left side, before the canine, there was an extra incisor. It reminded her again that this was no token, no symbol. This was bone that had lived; it had possessed a name and history. The old man continued to chant as, in confusion, Rose once more made her way back down the stairs.

Behind the song that Ishakak sings, Henry can hear the wind. He can hear the wind, and he can feel the snow that piles up outside the mission. The storm reaches across thousands of miles of the Arctic. Ishakak explained to him how these winds began where the god Nartsuk shook out his tunic of cariboo skin and let loose the air. The blizzard is blowing across the frozen ocean and over the snow houses of the people a mile or so from the mission, the weather now too fierce for anyone to move from one to the other. But for the last week, the hunting has been good. Henry prayed to his God, and Ishakak to his, and one or the other answered; there was enough meat in the houses of the people. Ishakak has sent Tornaq to him with a gift of cariboo.

The light of the coal-oil lantern is a deep gold, and somewhere, a draft comes in that makes the lantern sway a little. The mission is a ship at sea. The earth is rushing away beneath it, and he and Tornaq might be the last survivors in the wreck, waiting for fate to strike. Across the room she sits perfectly still, and her eyes are soft and full of something that he needs and fears. He knows that he ought to be praying, but he has no access to prayer; he is too far from land. The mission has left everything behind, like a tranced shaman on his way to the Land of the Dead or rising on the sled of Tarqip inua, the Moon Spirit, and swept across the sky. For weeks, Henry has been like a stone, unable to move, anchored to the earth, frozen, immobile, and now, suddenly, he is flying in the air and afraid that he has left his God and Jesus somewhere behind him, so that he is in the hands of other gods, Aningap and the terrible Ululiarnaq with her knife and bowl, who slits open the belly and tears out the entrails.

The light of the lamp fills the whole room with a golden oil, and both of them are bathed in it; if he moves, the movement will be slow and slippery, half incapable, as if they were drowning in the heavy light. First he was a stone, impassive, eternal, and now he is something else, something unknown and dangerous and desirable, something slow and lovely and endless and sweet. His bones cry out with fear and pain that they are being brought to life again, and he is afraid of what Tornaq sees when she looks at his face. He remembers her noises, the rhythmic grunts and cries and moans she made as Henry lay in the tent beside her and her husband, pretending to sleep as they took their pleasure. He had never imagined a woman making sounds like that. She smiles, and he feels himself disappearing; he is as light as air, and he may start to float around the room, this bouncing ship at sea. She is smiling, and he knows that the smile is reflected on his face. Childish and silly.

Tornaq stands up, and her wide face is brighter when it is closer to the lamp that hangs over her. Henry stands up too, and he seems to have trouble keeping his footing as the room heaves with the heaving of the ship. Tornaq reaches towards the lamp, and as she does, he stumbles, the lamp is out, and in the darkness they are close together and laughing.

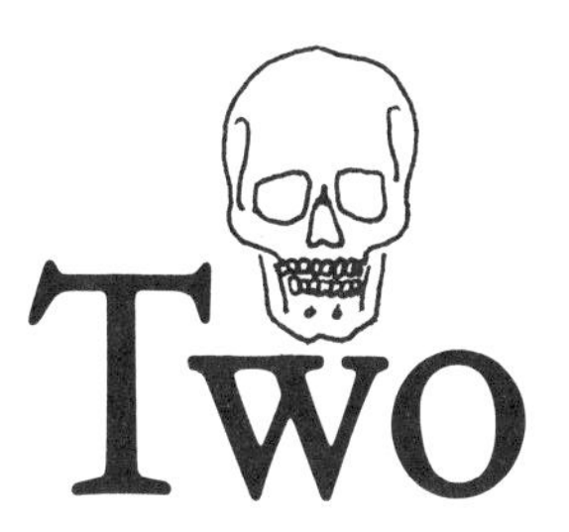
Two

The flesh is torn. The mouth opens to scream, but the sound is not heard, for there is no one to hear it. There is only the endless space of the empty landscape, treeless, ready for darkness. Life lives by death. The harpoon sinks in the flesh, and the pain becomes the one fact which is prior to any other fact. It is impossible to communicate pain, but easy to give it. There is no word large enough for this solitude, for the loneliness that is beyond loneliness, for the state of soul in which the word *impassive* is a description of paradise. Here time is only a procession of locked seconds. The flesh is transparent, and the figure enthroned is nebulous and grotesque. What is offered as comfort becomes the subtlest butchery, the steel edge separating muscle from bone; the body is a challenge to the skill of the knife. Words have abnegated. There are nameless things that some call stone, moss, water, but each of these names is an alias adopted for purposes of deception. The magic names have been lost. Love has lost its magic name and travels under the name of murder. It is one more way of tearing the flesh. Small fish eat tiny marine creatures, and larger fish eat smaller fish, and seals eat larger fish, and bears and men eat seals. This is called the great chain of being. At the top is God who eats everything in sight. We are all nourished on the Blood of the Lamb. One lamb or another.

Henry lay helpless; something had come loose in his brain. He was immersed now, not in water in which he could rot back to some natural state, become the mud that would grow new life, but in some cold noxious chemical that preserved him as a specimen, ready for dissection, and the mind had turned to an instrument to assault the cadaver. He had no resistance to the ache that spread from his shoulder, and the paralysis was a trap, as if he were tied down to be tortured.

Rock, moss, water, bone. A skull. The flesh torn away, eaten by gulls and crows, by foxes, by the wind. Rock, moss, water, bone. There was the emptiness that she left, and the emptiness that she found; he searched for hours, but there was nothing to be seen but the empty earth and empty sky. Rock, moss, water, bone. As the night came down, he knew that he too was lost, and that the two of them would walk forever across the silent space of the land, like spirits of the dead. He would lie down on the hard ground, and if it was too cold, he would die, and perhaps she would die too, at the same moment, and they would meet in heaven.

There was a figure near him, watching. It came to him and spoke Inuktitut; could show him the way back, even in the dark. He turned away and tried to see across the land where the sun had gone and the night shadow was heavy, and he wanted to cry out so that wherever she was lost, she might hear him and know that he had spent the day searching for her, that he wished to die when she did. His mouth opened but the sound that came was thin and poor, attenuated, useless. He let Tornaq guide him back to the mission, unable to understand how the Inuit woman could find her way in the dark; he followed obediently as a dog, he even chewed the piece of seal meat that she offered him, his feet and his jaws working together, mechanically. Tornaq did not speak when they got back to the mission, but instead turned and was lost in the blackness, and he went inside and sat in the dark, where all he could do was to say over and over to himself the familiar, helpless words: *O Lamb of God that takest away the sin of the world, have mercy upon us. O Lamb of God that takest away the sin of the world, have mercy upon us. O Lamb of God that takest away the sin of the world, grant us thy peace.*

When the light came back, his voice was only a hoarse whisper, and he got up and went back out the door and began to walk once again, to look for her, until he saw the clouds of a storm approaching from the west. To stay out in this would be to choose death. He climbed to a small hilltop and called her name over and over again, but the sound vanished. He stood still, exhausted. Again there was a figure watching him. Ishakak came towards him. When he reached the little hill where Henry was standing, he came up most of the way, then stopped a few feet short of the top. He stood in silence for a long time. Henry tried to find words to say; he was the missionary; he was supposed to have wisdom. Ishakak looked at him.

"She was tired," Ishakak said. "She wanted to go to the Moon Spirit right away. If you want to go there with her, I could help you hang yourself."

Henry turned and walked away, back towards the mission. The wind was growing stronger, and he could feel that the storm was close. Once the storm came, there could no longer be any hope that she might be found. He stopped, turned, looked all about him. He could see for miles in the vivid air under the dark clouds, and it seemed that he must discover her somewhere. Nothing. Nothing but the rolling land, and a blue arm of the sea, and in the distance, the fearful bulk of the mountains.

Henry could not make himself move. To move, to turn back, was to abandon her. Yet he had no idea where to look, which way to turn. For a long time, he stared at the small stones by his feet, as if they might speak and tell him what to do. He ought to pray. When he tried, the only words he could find were *into thy hands*, and he repeated them over and over in his head as if they were, not a prayer, but a magic formula; the words were Christ's, and he wondered if his use of them might be blasphemous, but he was beyond such distinctions.

The wind was gusting hard now, and he began to walk back to the mission, and once he had begun, he went without stopping. He passed the empty Hudson's Bay store, climbed the small hill. At the door of the mission, he turned, looked at Ishakak and met his eyes for the first time.

"She was tired," Ishakak said. "She went to the Moon Spirit."

Henry couldn't speak, just stumbled into the small building and walked to the table at the front which he used for serving communion. Over it hung a crucifix, and Henry knelt in front of the table and began to repeat prayers, forcing himself to remember the words, bringing his mind to some kind of focus on this act of recall. He prayed until he could remember no more prayers. The room was silent but outside he could hear the wind and the snow driving against the windows of the mission.

Albert Press was due back soon. He was the clerk at the Hudson's Bay store and he had gone up the coast in an RCMP boat to act as interpreter. Perhaps, somehow, those in the boat would see her walking near the shore and bring her back. Henry went and looked out the window. She couldn't survive this storm.

He went to the bedroom and looked once more to see if she might have left him a note, something. It was foolish to expect it; she had been gone from him a long time. He'd never understood why she had decided to come to the Arctic with him, and on the boat that brought them in, he could feel her retiring inside herself. Once they had arrived, there was silence, and from time to time, in despair, he had almost wished to be free of it. Perhaps she had understood that he longed to be free from the painful silence in which there were only hard memories. She had gone. She was out there somewhere in the storm, and soon enough she would be invisible. It was not sinful of her to have chosen death; it was Henry's fault that he could not reach her, that he couldn't say the words that needed to be said, that he had forced her to choose. If only he could believe that she had gone to Wilf, that by some magic, a boat or an aeroplane had appeared at the inlet with a figure waving to her, and that she had run to escape to the arms of her lover.

But in the Arctic, no one came for you. You were alone with your distress. Letters arrived once a year, if the ice broke early enough for the boat to get through. There was no place to run to except the barren country, the sea, the mountains.

Henry should not have brought her here. He should have sent her away with her lover. He remembered his pleasure when she had decided to come north with him; he thought it would be a new beginning for them, but that was, he knew now, only fantasy mixed with a perverse joy in what seemed his conquest. He believed she had chosen him. He didn't let himself notice how far from him she had gone, that they never touched. As he stared into this first of the winter's storms, he tried to imagine where she was, tried to send his spirit out to accompany her, to share her dying.

As the moment of her death came close to him, he began to know what it had been like for her to be here, alone, with no one to talk to, no comfort. She had always been easily frightened, and she hated all the death, the butchery and blood that were taken for granted. These people lived by killing, their constant acts of propitiation acknowledged this, but for her it was unbearable to see a seal harpooned, its body, still alive, flopping on the ice, or dragged dead across the snow, a fat lump with an oddly human face. To see the hands of one of the women crimson as she cut apart the flesh of the seal and drew out the long string of the intestines. To see a young Inuit boy, not much more than a toddler, stoning to death a seagull he had caught in a snare. She had not been trained for this. Even Henry had been startled by the smell of the houses, the closeness, the offhand performance of bodily functions.

At night, in bed, they would hear the dogs howling. She wouldn't let him touch her. She was frightened that she might become pregnant and have to bear a child here in the wilderness.

Her mouth, he knew now, had been stifling a scream. The lines of her face had been altered in some indefinable way, like a picture that is slowly going out of focus; behind the skin, sorrow gathered and with this accumulation of distress, the features changed, but the change was subtle, almost invisible, and he had chosen not to understand it. Love was useless without knowledge, and he had chosen not to know her pain, had perhaps been unable to know it. When Christ counselled men to love one another, he didn't offer a way of understanding the secrecy, the difficult inner life of the others who were to be loved.

When they were on their way into the Arctic, the ship that was bringing them became trapped in the ice, and for days they were unable to move. It wasn't clear whether a shift in wind might release them, and if it did, whether the boat might not have to turn back. He had stood beside Amelia one afternoon when the sky in the east grew red, and it seemed that they were watching the approach of some huge conflagration, a whole city in flames, but it was only an effect of the light; out of the flames rose the round globe of the full moon, and the fire vanished.

"The boat might have to go back," he said. It was the first time he had spoken the words to her, and she turned and looked at him. The look was long and profound; he seemed to be seeing into the soul of the woman who faced him, and yet he didn't understand what it was he saw. It was powerful, even terrifying, but he had no comprehension of it. He could only guess.

That moment, locked in the ice, the two of them silent together under the rising moon that had left behind its mirage of incandescence, was both transparent and opaque. It seemed to contain the past and the future, and yet it offered nothing by way of help, of explanation. She might have spoken then; she might have told him what she felt. He wondered sometimes if he had the right to anger that she would not explain her suffering; perhaps she herself couldn't comprehend it, or perhaps she felt she had no right to complain. Could it be that the whole doctrine of love fell afoul of our ignorance and blindness? It was a philosophical question, and philosophy was a discipline for which he had always felt contempt. It offered neither truth nor help. Theology offered help at least.

But what if help meant nothing without truth?

Where was God while Amelia sank into the cold ocean of her distress? The answer must be that God was there if she looked, and if she chose not to seek Him, she could not expect to find Him. It was one more thing that Henry did not know, whether she might have prayed and struggled. Only he remembered how she looked at the communion rail, poised and still, her hand touching the silver cup as the wine reached her lips, her face lovely and prayerful.

Outside the mission, the wind was louder, and in the distance, over the gasps of the blizzard, he could hear the dogs howling from the tents of the people further along the shore. He couldn't escape the superstitious fear that they were howling because this was the moment of Amelia's death. He tried to pray for her to go easily, even happily, but the universe was resistant to his prayer. From the steamer trunk that they used as furniture, he pulled out one of the small drawers. Inside were some of her clothes, and he took them out; a pullover, knitted socks, a cardigan, and laid them on the bed. The red pullover was one that she had knitted for herself in the country parsonage where they had spent three years. He lay on the bed and held the sweater against his face and cried.

Henry opened his eyes; these memories were too much. He looked at the figure of Ishakak beside the bed. The old man had stopped chanting now and was smoking his pipe, his eyes turned out the window, focused on the distance, as if he could see for miles, though Henry knew there was nothing there but a tree and, beyond it, a view of the brick wall of the house across the street. The eyes of the angakok weren't limited by the bounds of reality.

How had Ishakak known of his illness? And why had he come? Curiosity? Helpfulness? The desire to triumph over Henry? Probably all of those; he was never a simple man. Henry had never been sure why he had sent Tornaq to him. No doubt she had wanted to come to the missionary; she'd been making eyes at Henry since his arrival, and as his grasp of Inuktitut improved, he began to understand the jokes she made, which were not always very proper.

Ishakak never attended the church services. Some of the others attended, enjoyed themselves and left, apparently untouched. One couple who were regular and enthusiastic hymn singers had refused to be baptised, explaining that if they did, they would have to give up spouse exchanges. Ishakak kept his distance. Yet he was friendly, even eager to help, especially when it came to explaining the beliefs of his people.

Henry remembered once in the long winter night when he sat in Ishakak's snow house while the man told him about the taboos. Each time he was told one, Henry would ask why? Ishakak ignored the question and went on with his explanation. Again Henry would ask why? Finally, Ishakak began to put on his parka, indicating that Henry should do the same. He led the way outside where three men were coming back from hunting, the blizzard blowing all around them. They had spent hours on the sea ice, but not one of them had a seal. They were hungry and tired. Ishakak pointed to them, talked of their hunger, how for hours the blizzard had blown in their faces while they hunted. Why? he asked. Why?

He led Henry to another snow house where Tikirluk nursed a sick baby. Her husband had recently died, and even before that, he had been a poor hunter and they had often been hungry. Why? he asked Henry. Why?

Henry understood, and they made their way back to Ishakak's house where Tornaq would brew the tea that Henry had brought as a gift. These people lived in a world of arbitrary circumstance. They lived and died by the behaviour of the weather, the cariboo, the seals. And in the face of this arbitrary fate, they had constructed an intricate system of taboos. Their world was chaotic, and so were their beliefs. Perhaps only men who had power over their world could conceive of a systematic theology.

No. The language men used reflected their world, but they had the power to reach beyond it. They must. There was something beyond that sought expression in the world of men.

Something beyond; something within. There was a story he had been told in the North about shamanic power coming on a woman. She had gone out of the snow house to make water when she saw a glowing ball of fire in the sky coming towards her. She could not flee and the light entered her. She felt herself full of it and she lost consciousness. When she woke, she possessed the powers of an angakok.

Henry came back to the mission and told Amelia, and when he had finished, he couldn't understand the look on her face until she spoke. To her it was the same story as Paul on the road to Damascus. Henry had tried to convince her that it was not the same, that one was a pagan illusion while the other was divine illumination, and when she had challenged him to define the difference, he had said, by their fruits. The one led to trick healing, meaningless seances, and the other to the missionary activities of Paul, his great expression of the Christian truths.

She had stopped arguing with him then. He had suggested that they pray together, and she had acceded, and Henry had believed that was enough, but now he understood how deeply doubt had gone into her, that perhaps she had been driven to walk into the mountains or the sea not only by a personal emptiness but also by the loss of the voice of God.

He looked for a moment at the skull beside his bed, then away, quickly. He wanted to know where Ishakak had found it, how long he had carried it with him, but he couldn't bring himself to scribble the questions on his pad. When Ishakak began to speak Inuktitut, Henry had felt for a moment that he himself would be able to speak it, though he was dumb in English. But no words came.

Perhaps he should tell Rose to send Ishakak away. She would do it for him, and he would not have to see the skull beside his bed, the teeth that had never grown old but were still the teeth of the young woman he had loved. It filled him with terror to see them.

The passage from the bishop's house to the cathedral was

dim, with one bulb at each end, and it was always cool and damp, like a cave, even in the hot weather. Rose was going to make the initial measurements for the shelves and cupboards of the cathedral archive. To get underway was increasingly urgent, she felt. If the bishop didn't begin to improve soon, he would be sent into retirement and another put in his place.

Or there was the other possibility. Ishakak's words, so blunt and untroubled, came back to her. *You can't fix somebody when he wants to die.* Rose didn't like to admit that they expressed her own feeling that Henry was eager to go away from them all, into whatever was made ready for him. She hated the idea; perhaps that meant her faith was poor, but there was nothing to be done about that. She would create the archive because he had wished it, and quickly, before someone else could countermand the wish.

As she reached the far end, she could see the daylight that fell from the marine provisioner's window. Had he known that his window would end in this obscure corner of the building, presiding over a tunnel? Perhaps he had been a man of questionable morals, and the cathedral clergy of his time had preferred to have his memorial window out of sight.

The door led into a back corridor near the choir room, and as she opened it, Rose saw two figures in the doorway a few feet away. They stopped talking and looked towards her. It was Gordon Budge, the cathedral organist, and Elaine Heverson, the chairman of the choir guild. Elaine turned rather abruptly away from Gordon and came towards Rose. She was a spindly woman, brittle and quick, but with large breasts that hung heavily on her narrow chest, looking misplaced and pathetic, and a small fleshy growth on the side of her nose that sorted oddly with a striking face, huge grey eyes and a wide, perfectly shaped mouth, the bones of a fashion model.

"Let's ask Rose," Elaine said. "I bet she'll agree with me."

"Don't ask Rose," Rose said. "Rose doesn't settle arguments."

Gordon was a small man with a fluffy beard, unmarried and assumed by most to be homosexual. He had his points, Rose had always thought, including the fact that he lent her his small station wagon to haul lumber, but she had said to herself the first time she saw him walk past that he had an insolent bum, and she had decided since that the rest of him matched.

A month ago, Gordon had come to the bishop looking for support for his proposal to raise money for the cathedral choir by doing a performance of *Don Giovanni* with the women's parts played by the choirboys. He insisted that Peter Gruending, his treble soloist, would make a wonderful Donna Anna, and that putting the boys in eighteenth-century women's gowns was no more absurd than the frills and cassocks they usually wore. Even the bishop had been reduced to stunned silence by this.

"What we were arguing about," Elaine said, ignoring Rose's refusal to arbitrate, "was a new piece of music for the special service for the bishop."

"I haven't heard anything about that," Rose said.

"The dean's planning a service of prayer for the bishop's recovery."

"No one mentioned it."

"I was telling Gordon that he should write a special anthem. I always take notes on the bishop's sermons, and I have pages of quotations where he could find a wonderful text."

"And Gordon considers it beneath him, is that it?"

Rose was inclined to like Gordon, but she did find him smug, and she enjoyed teasing and tumbling him whenever she got the opportunity.

"Gordon has quite enough to do running the choir and playing the organ for services, without having to write music as well," he said.

"Bach managed."

"I'm not Bach."

"That's an uncharacteristically humble comment," Rose said. "Are you unwell?"

"I've never understood, Rose, why you treat me as a punching bag."

"Why don't you write the piece?" Rose said. "The bishop's been good to you."

"I'm not a composer."

"What about that anthem last month?"

"Once a year, maybe twice, I scribble a few bars. But I can't just turn out something on order."

"But Gordon, it's such a nice idea," Elaine said. "Everyone would be so pleased."

There was something in her manner that startled Rose, something almost intimate, as if it presumed on a shared privacy. Had her son Gregory become Gordon's favourite? It was assumed that Gordon had the good taste to keep his hands off the choirboys, but since the Don Giovanni proposal, Rose was prepared to question Gordon's good taste. He had, after all, proposed that he would play Don Giovanni and, if she remembered correctly, suggested that Gregory Heverson play Zerlina. *La ci darem la mano,* Greg. Rose began to feel a little dizzy as some of the more extraordinary possibilities of the situation opened up in front of her. She preferred not knowing too much about human relationships; they were a quagmire.

"As I said, Elaine, I don't settle arguments. You'll have to work it out on your own."

Rose walked away from them to the empty room she'd come to measure. From the pocket of her dress, she took the tape measure and a small notebook. She wouldn't try to make any plans at first, just measure the room and sketch its proportions, then later transfer these to graph paper and use that as a basis for some sketches. She wanted to make something splendid though she didn't dare put out the money for hardwood for everything. She'd have to use plywood for the doors and counters. That meant birch or mahogany. Mahogany was probably more suitable for a church. Damned mahogany. She should have been born a century earlier when it was possible to get hold of decent woods.

Rose measured the room carefully, walls, floors, windows, doorway, the placing of the heating vent in the floor. She enjoyed getting it right, opening up the potential for the room to become something else. She must get Chappie the sexton to show her the boxes of old books and papers and then decide how much shelving was needed and what kind of drawers and cupboards. It would take her a while to design and build the archive. And there was the bird-cage she wanted to finish. She put away her measuring tape and notebook.

To reach Chappie's room, she had to go through the cathedral and down the front steps. In some ways, the building, with its various offshoots and attachments, was like a maze, built in unplanned bursts, straggling and incoherent; there was no direct connection between the tunnel to the diocesan centre and the main cathedral basement. As Rose walked along a narrow corridor towards the body of the church, she saw Gordon and Elaine, down another hall, entering the choir room, Elaine still talking urgently. The way for her to convince Gordon, Rose suspected, was flattery, and not too subtle. Rose opened the door that led into the north transept, and as always, she was both startled and lightened in spirit by the size and height of the building, the lovely filtered daylight that was everywhere, the way the eye was lifted towards the bright blue dome. The rows of dark pews in the nave were empty, the kneelers neatly folded up. She could hear her own footsteps echo softly through the space as she made her way to the cathedral entrance. There was a room there for the sidesmen, and at the back of it a large door that led to the basement.

As she walked through the cathedral, she remembered what the bishop had told her about George Herbert making subjects for poems out of the commonplace features of the church building, the lock and key, the church floor, the windows. If Rose had been able to make a poem, it would have been about the way the cathedral contained space, making it something more than emptiness, yet not imprisonment. That was what a church ought to be, a place where the soul could expand to a wider horizon, where the soul itself could become spacious and serene.

The door to the basement was open, and the light at the bottom was turned on. It was sometimes suggested that Chappie spent too much of his time in the sexton's room while Bill, his helper, did most of the work, but the two of them seemed amicable enough, and the cleaning got done, so the matter was left to rest.

When Rose reached the door of Chappie's room, she saw him, with a cup of tea and a cigarette, bent over a book. It was a paperback collection of little known facts. Chappie had a substantial collection of these, and several sets of old encyclopedias, bought second-hand. He had a fierce will to educate himself, education in his mind meaning the mastery of a panoply of recalcitrant facts. He appeared to believe that it was possible to know everything, if you got enough encyclopedias and worked at them with sufficient enthusiasm. However Chappie's brain was a resistant organ, and his memory was poor. He would stun you with a little known fact one day, but it would be gone a week later. An intensity and anger grew from this desperate battle to control the chaos of phenomena that would never submit to his efforts. He was a Sisyphus among autodidacts, and somewhere in him was the fatal knowledge that he would never win.

"What do you call a group of doves, Rose? Do you know that?"

"No, Chappie, I have no idea."

"A dule. A dule of doves."

"I've never heard that."

"What about crows?"

"A flock of crows."

"No."

"I've always said a flock of crows."

"A *murder* of crows."

"No."

"That's what it says here."

"It sounds strange to me. I think I'm more at home with questions like what's the longest river in the world."

Chappie looked towards her, the cigarette hanging from his heavy lips, smoke curling up towards his eyes which looked suddenly suspicious. He thought she was challenging him to name the longest river, and he was searching wildly for the correct answer.

"What I really need to know, Chappie, is where to find all the old books and papers that the bishop wants sorted and saved."

He was still staring at her.

"It's not the Mississippi," he said.

"I think it's the Nile," Rose said. "Or the Amazon."

"It's in here somewhere," Chappie said and began to turn pages.

"Show me these books and things first," Rose said, "and then you can look it up."

Irritably, Chappie stubbed out his cigarette in the old metal tray in front of him and drank down the last of the tea.

"I know it's not the Mississippi," he said, and he led the way out of the small room, crowded with pails and brooms and bottles of cleanser. He went to a door a few feet away. From his pocket, he took a large ring of keys, and after a moment of contemplation, he selected one of them and unfastened the padlock.

"It's in here," he said. "Mostly rubbish if you ask me."

He dragged open the door. Inside it was so dark that Rose could see nothing. There was a smell of mildew.

"Is there a light?" she said.

"I'll have to plug in the extension."

In a few moments he was back with a work-light, a bulb in a wire cage on the end of a long orange cord.

"I'll lock the door behind me when I'm finished," Rose said. Chappie walked away without speaking, and she carried the work-light into the room. She noticed a couple of old trunks, some wooden bins and piles of cardboard boxes; she'd have a quick look today, but she'd have to come back later to make an accurate inventory of what was here. Rose opened one of the boxes in front of her. It was full of old books. She lifted one out. It had a cover of a dim greenish colour, cracked down the back. There was no title page, and the opening pages of the text were missing, but inside the cover, someone had written in pencil: *The Commonplaces of Peter Martyr, referred to by Milton in his prose work* Tetrachordon. *Peter Martyr, an able theologian of Italy, was brought to England by Cranmer and made professor of theology at Oxford in 1549.*

Rose let the book fall open in her hand. The print, with its archaic spelling and long s's and f's, looked to be of the seventeenth century. Two thirds of the way down the page was a question in italics: *"What is eternall death?"* Beneath was the answer:

> It is the unspeakable, most wretched, most fearfull, and endlesse condition of the Reprobate, ordained by God: not in that the soule may again be separated from the bodie, or that the bodie, or soule dyeth, and that they cease either to bee, to liue, to have sense (for they shall bee, and shall live continually): but in that they shall bee for euer shut out both in soule and bodie, not onely from all fauour and beholding the presence of God, but also that they shall bee adiudged most iustly to an horrible endlesse and deserued curse, by reason of their sinne.

Rose closed the book and put it down. It was chilling. Only the primitive believed in damnation any more, at least in those terms. Was it Graham Greene who said, There is a hell but there is no one in it? But who was to say that the modern sentimentalists were more right than the traditional sadists?

She heard a noise and turned. Chappie stood in the doorway behind her.

"The Nile," he said. "Four thousand, one hundred and eighty miles long."

"You were right," she said. "It wasn't the Mississippi."

He was gone. Rose examined a couple more books. *The Works of Richard Hooker: Of the Laws of Ecclesiastical Polity*. A narrative of a missionary journey through Africa. She took out her tape. This box held enough books to fill two-and-a-half feet of shelf space. She glanced around the room and counted. Something like sixty feet of bookshelves, she estimated. Rose lifted the lid of one of the trunks. It contained a few books, and some old ledgers, and what appeared to be school work books. She closed the trunk, unable to confront those documents of vanished lives, not today, not with Peter Martyr's description of damnation ringing in her ears. It was always dangerous for Rose to be aware of the human past, how many others had lived on earth, that they were weak and hurt and foolish as she was. Thousands had died believing that they might be going to an endless torment because they had not given satisfaction to their God, and yet each one had clung desperately to the facts of a daily life which soon enough would be lost forever in the pitiless cycle of time. It was too much for her to think about. History, the multiplicity of the past, was a flood that drowned her soul.

Rose left the room, locked the door behind her. She turned towards the spaces of the dusty cathedral cellar that stretched in front of her, like the dark photographic negative of the graceful space above. Rose lifted the work-light, thought she saw something move, but when she studied the dim vista, she could see nothing but piles of chairs, boxes, benches, organ pipes. It was probably a wild cat that lived down here, perhaps a family of them breeding and inbreeding.

Rose snapped off the work-light and rolled the extension cord as she carried it back to Chappie's office. He was gone now, his paperback, tea cup and ashtray sitting under the bare bulb on the old card table.

Instead of going back into the offices behind the north transept and the choir, Rose went out the front door into daylight. There were dark storm clouds blowing in from the west, and gusts of wind tossing the flowers in their beds. She crossed the lawn to the old brick house where the bishop lay silent. She needed to talk to him. She needed to know why men should be shut out both in body and soul from beholding the presence of God.

He would not tell her. That or anything.

As Rose entered the house and walked towards the bishop's office, she heard the sounds of argument. The only voice she recognized immediately was that of Frank Neal, the bishop's executive assistant. When she reached the door, she saw there were three figures in the office, Frank Neal, Canon Stan Butts, and Edgar Worral, who was the most influential member of the diocesan executive. When she walked in, they all rose from their chairs.

"Sit back down," Rose said. "I'm not the Queen. Or even the Archbishop of Canterbury."

Frank didn't like jokes when he was looking businesslike. Rose went to her desk. Edgar Worral, who wore an expensive dark blue suit and looked, with his neatly trimmed white beard, professionally handsome, turned to her.

"What ever possessed you to let him in?"

"Who?"

"This witch doctor."

"He said he wanted to see the bishop."

"And if a drunk from one of the local bars asked to see the bishop, would you let him in?"

"What is this?" Rose asked. "The Spanish Inquisition?"

"I don't understand why you let him in."

"He'd come all the way from the Arctic. Obviously he knew the bishop when he was in the North."

"Frank says you found this Eskimo sitting on the front steps and you took him directly to the bishop."

"And I asked the bishop if he wanted to see him, and the bishop said he did."

"The bishop's in no state to be making decisions like that."

"Henry Wade is still in charge of this diocese. Until he chooses to retire or is replaced by the archbishop, he can perfectly well decide what he wants and doesn't want."

"But, Rose," Stan Butts said, "we can't really have this Eskimo sitting up there chanting."

He sounded as if he might be about to cry. He was famous for the ease of his weeping. From time to time he was seen serving communion with tears rolling down his face, and he never went into the pulpit without two clean handkerchiefs.

"Don't start to blubber, Stanley," Ed Worral said.

"I'm not. And don't treat me like an idiot, Edgar. You know perfectly well that it's only beautiful things make me cry. The eucharist and little children and the love of God."

"Well there's nothing beautiful about this bloody Eskimo."

"I thought he was quite handsome," Rose said.

Frank turned and gave her a hard look. She wasn't being helpful.

"I think we're agreed," Frank said, "that he can't just stay here."

"I imagine he'll soon want to leave," Rose said.

"That's not what he says," Frank snapped.

"What does he say?"

"That he's going to stay with Henry until he dies. That's what he told the nurse. And he's been eating all the food that Henry leaves on the tray."

"Why don't we prepare a tray for him?" Rose asked.

"Don't do that!" Ed Worral said. "It will just encourage him."

"Starve them out. The British army found that used to work with the Indians, didn't they, Ed?"

Edgar Worral was a retired military officer. He took the remark badly.

"Perhaps we should move to your office, Frank."

"I think Rose should be involved in the decision. She's been the closest to the bishop, in many ways."

"Since Rose let him in, why don't we leave it to Rose to get him out?"

"Rose will get him out when the bishop decides he doesn't want him there," Rose said firmly.

"Are we sure the bishop is . . . alert," Stan Butts said.

"He appears to be able to understand," Frank said, "but he doesn't show much interest in things. Since he left the hospital he seems depressed. The doctor says it's not uncommon."

"But he knows what he's doing?"

"Yes," Rose said, "he does."

"I can't believe that Henry understands that he's making the whole diocese look foolish," Ed Worral said.

"The bishop has never been one to worry about appearances," Frank said.

"So I've noticed. But this is too much."

"Why?" Rose said.

"We are members of the Christian church. We are all officers of this Anglican diocese. Our bishop is lying mute and paralyzed. And some pagan witch doctor is conducting services. It's not appropriate. It's probably blasphemous." Worral paused for breath. "I understand

Curwan Brant offered to come in and pray with him in the afternoons. That would be much more suitable."

"Curwan would finish him off in a week."

"Rose," Stan Butts said, "that's unfair."

"It may be unfair," Rose said, "but it's not untrue." She was beginning to realize that she was talking herself out of a job. It was unlikely that the bishop was going to get better, and without his support, Rose would be removed from the diocesan office with all the suddenness of a mummified corpse being hoisted out to heaven at the last trumpet. It was too late to worry about it now.

Frank sat up a little higher in his chair. He was about to become chairman of this unofficial meeting.

"There are a number of questions that have to be settled. The first one is whether the bishop's decision, assuming he wants this man to stay, is to be accepted as the final one."

"All we have to do," Edgar said, "is phone the archbishop. He'll see how absurd this is, and Henry will have to take his orders."

"It's a personal matter," Rose said. "The bishop, like any other man, should have the right to choose those who keep him company during his illness."

"Since he has no family," Frank said, "the church could be said to stand in the place of his family."

"*In loco parentis*?" Rose said.

"Not exactly," Frank said.

"Is that some RC doctrine?" Worral said.

"No, Edgar," Stan Butts said patiently. "It means in

the place of parents. It's what the university is to its students."

"Used to be," Rose said. "They object to that now."

"As I said, the church is the only family that Henry has."

"That's no reason for the church to begin to act like a wicked stepmother."

"We have to have some concern for decency," Worral said. "I'm not just speaking for myself. I canvassed other members of the executive committee by phone."

"And told them you were going to war against a pagan witch doctor."

"I told them the situation."

"If you'd said Henry was having a visit from an old friend, do you think they'd have wanted to throw Ishakak out?"

"If I'd told them that, it wouldn't have been the truth."

"It certainly would."

"We don't seem to be getting anywhere," Frank said.

"Perhaps we should call a meeting of the whole executive committee," Stan Butts said.

"Do that and the next thing you'll have it in the newspaper," Ed Worral said. He was beginning to sweat, and he took out a brilliantly white handkerchief and rubbed his forehead.

"I agree," Rose said. "There's no need for any more meetings."

"As long as something's done. We don't want this

Eskimo turning up at this special service the dean's planning."

Rose wondered if Elaine had succeeded in persuading Gordon to write the anthem. Would she bribe him? Offer to let him take Greg to the movies? Surely not.

Edgar was rubbing his forehead again. His face was red, and Rose was afraid they might soon have another stroke victim on their hands. The argument subsided for a moment, and there was a moment of quiet in which Rose heard the sound of Ishakak chanting from the room upstairs.

"He's at it right now!" Worral said.

"He's singing," Rose said. "Henry may find it comforting. People like to be sung to when they're ill."

"That's not music."

"It certainly sounds rather wanton," Stan said.

"He's performing some kind of ceremony," Worral said.

"What if he is?"

"Ecumenism is all very fine, but I don't think anyone ever suggested including witch doctors. Not even Henry."

"He's not a witch doctor. He's a shaman."

"Fancy word for the same thing."

"Perhaps if he stayed somewhere else," Stan Butts said. "Out of the road. The basement."

"With Rose's machinery," Worral said, with nasty irony.

"We really must sort this out," Frank said. He was accustomed to being the voice of common sense and always being able to find common ground. He didn't like absurdities.

"There's nothing to sort out," Rose said, "so long as we realize that the bishop is as intelligent as he ever was, and as capable of making decisions. Frank can explain the problem to him, and he can decide."

"If you're sure he knows . . ."

"Stan, none of the doctors has ever suggested that he's lost his marbles. He just can't talk."

"Maybe we could at least convince Ishakak to put away that skull," Frank said.

"What skull?"

"He has a human skull sitting on the table with his other bits and pieces."

"This gets worse and worse," Worral said.

"It's one of the exercises of the angakok," Rose said. She'd been doing some reading. "They stare at bones, especially a skull. It helps them to see into the heart of life. To be a shaman, you have to be able to see your own skeleton through the flesh. It's not that much different from the monks who used to keep a skull on their table as a *memento mori.*"

"I thought we'd abandoned that kind of thing at the reformation."

"We abandoned monasticism, Edgar. Not the contemplation of death."

"This is no time for theological argument," Frank said. "We have a practical problem to be solved."

"You know my opinion," Edgar Worral said as he got

up from his chair. "I'll leave it to you Frank, and I'll call tomorrow to see what you've done."

"Fine," Frank said, doing his best to sound cheerful about the whole thing. He walked with Edgar Worral towards the front door. Stan Butts turned to Rose.

"I know it's unfashionable to say so, Rose, but there *are* powers, spiritual powers. They've been known to be dangerous."

"The bishop knows more about that than we do."

Stan looked at her for a long time.

"Has he ever talked to you about his time in the Arctic?"

"No. Just to say he was there."

"He never talks to anyone about it."

"Maybe he has nothing to say."

"I don't think that's the reason," Stan said.

"He lost his wife there."

"Perhaps it's only that, too painful to remember, but if so, why would he want it brought back now? Why would he want that Eskimo fellow to be with him?"

"I don't know why, Stan. But I want him to have what he wants."

"You're very loyal, Rose. I admire that."

His eyes were growing damp as he turned and looked out the window. The sky was covered with clouds.

"It's blowing up a storm out there. I'd better get my bicycle home before it starts to pour."

After he left the room, Rose shifted things idly around on her desk, then took out the measurements and began to transfer the sketches to graph paper. She would make the shelves and cupboards before they threw her out.

Henry listened to the rain falling outside his room. The night brought comfort. His mind slowed, and the eyes no longer sought out pain. It was like lying in his bedroom when he was a child, the sound of the rain on the roof and running down through the metal eaves bringing with it a kind of intoxication; he would imagine the animals huddled in their shelter, a groundhog under the earth, a rabbit beneath a pile of brush. The child wondered what the birds did in the rain, how they kept dry. The English sparrows hid under the eaves of the house, but what about the wild birds?

There were so many birds out there, so many animals that needed shelter and warmth that he worried that God couldn't take care of them all. Sometimes on rainy nights, he would put them in his prayers. After he had prayed for blessing on all those close to him, he would ask God to keep the animals from getting wet and cold.

Rain wasn't like that in the daytime. He would go out and play in a summer storm, laughing and dancing and waving at Alice-Alice who stood at the edge of the veranda and watched but refused to join him. Rain in the day could be a game, but rain at night was different; it made you think of people without houses, or the animals, their dark eyes hurt as the water soaked their fur.

They found Jasper Nash lying in the rain. In a ditch beside the road, with a hole in his head where Percy shot him. Everybody knew it must be Percy; the two brothers were always fighting when they were drunk, and once Percy had shot the windows out of Jasper's house.

It rained the night they hanged Percy Nash too. They tried to keep it a secret from Henry and Alice-Alice, but Henry found out. Their father had to be at the jail to watch. When Henry said his prayers that night, he prayed to God to keep the animals warm and dry and then he prayed for Percy Nash and climbed into bed. His mother looked down at him after he said that, and he could tell she was almost crying, but her face looked angry at the same time.

"Don't you be thinking about Percy Nash. You're too young for such things."

Then she kissed him and left the room, and Henry tried not to think about them hanging Percy Nash and his father being there to watch because he was Percy's lawyer, but he couldn't keep it out of his mind. He'd seen Percy Nash on the streets, but he couldn't remember him very well, and all he could think of was the picture they had of him in the paper. He imagined him hanging on the end of the rope, his face looking like that, but he knew the face would be different and horrible. Henry put his fingers around his throat and choked himself to see what it felt like. He scared himself, and almost started to cry, and he tried not to think about Percy, but he couldn't stop.

When he was walking back from school, he heard two men on the street talking about who built the gallows, and how you could hear the hammering from outside the jail.

Someone at school said that they sent the hangman from Toronto, specially to do it. Nobody knew who he was.

Henry's father would hate watching, but he would never say so. You could tell when he didn't like things, but he wasn't one to say what he was thinking. He didn't come home for dinner today, and their mother said he was busy at the office, but Henry knew it was because he didn't want to see them before he had to watch Percy Nash be hanged.

Percy was the first person they ever hanged in this jail. Someone at school said that. Henry wondered how many people would be there besides his father. The priest would be there, because Percy was RC, and Henry's father, and the hangman. Maybe somebody from the newspaper.

Henry couldn't stop thinking what it was like when he choked himself and how Percy would feel like that but worse; he would feel like that for a long time, until he was dead. One of the bigger kids at school said dirty things about what happened when they hanged you, and Henry started to think about that too, until he was so scared that he thought he'd start to cry and have to ask his mother to come and sit with him.

He tried to think of something nice, but he couldn't. There was the time when he was little and he stayed at his grandmother's house and she let him drink tea, but when he remembered that, he remembered that his grandmother was dead, and that started him thinking about choking and being dead. Henry thought it might help if he prayed, but he couldn't seem to find any words, until he thought of praying that Percy wouldn't feel it when the rope choked him. He wasn't sure if God could do that, but his mother said that God could do anything if He wanted.

Henry tried to listen to the rain, but it made him think of Jasper Nash lying dead in the rain and how Percy shot him. He put his head under his pillow and pretended that he was an animal in a warm den and God was looking after him. He hummed to himself "This Is My Father's World," and for a minute he thought it was going to be all right, but then the choking came back and the fear of what it was like to be dead. If Percy was a murderer, God would send him to Hell, so that even when the choking stopped and he was dead, then he'd wake up and be in Hell.

Henry took the pillow off his head and got up to go to the bathroom. He could see a light from the downstairs hall, but there was no sound. His mother must be reading or knitting. The light from the front room made a curve of brightness on the wallpaper, covered with small yellow flowers that Henry could never quite keep himself from counting as he made his way up the stairs to bed at night. Instead of going to the bathroom, Henry wanted to race down the stairs and run to where his mother sat, but he was afraid that if he did that, his father would come in, and Henry would have to turn and watch as the man took off his hat and shook the rain from it, and looking, he would know where his father had been, see the traces of the event on his face.

Henry walked quietly down the hall to the bathroom.

He flushed the toilet before he left, and though he knew his mother must have heard it, she didn't call out to him to ask why he was out of bed. Henry wondered if she was thinking of Percy Nash, and how it must feel to have the rope choking you. Henry got into bed, and somehow he slept, and when he woke, the whole house was dark, so he knew it was the middle of the night, and that it was over.

Sleep had come, as sleep comes, finally, to those lost moments of night, with the blessing of unconsciousness and the bizarre puzzles and inversions of dream. To all those lost moments: Henry lying on his side of the bed of the country parsonage, staring into the darkness, listening to the breathing of the woman who lay beside him. He was afraid that if he touched her, he would sense the presence of her lover, that there would be a spark, as when you touch a doorknob after walking on carpet. The lover must have left some charge of human electricity on her body. When she came in and shook the rain from the scarf that she had tied over her head, he could see it in the brightness of her eyes, the colour in her face that was too vivid to be produced only by the walk in the rain. Henry had been sitting in his chair with George Herbert's little prose work *The Country Parson* in his hand, his face turned down as if he were reading, his eyes unable to compass the words or his mind the meaning of the words. He had come back early from a meeting of the vestry council, and he had known, as soon as he had turned up the road towards the parsonage, that Amelia would not be there, that she was with her lover, hidden somewhere from the rain, perhaps in a barn or an empty garage. He had not called out when he came in the house, for he knew there would be no answer, and he had taken out Herbert's little book, which he loved for its sweet seriousness and passion. When Amelia came in the door, her bright eyes had turned to him and then turned away.

As they prepared for bed, Henry tried not to look at Amelia, lest he see marks that had been left on her body by the man's hands. She bruised easily, and he knew that there would be traces, little prints of passion. More than that, he could not bear the pain of wanting her, of wanting to cry out that he would share her, that he would take second place and content himself with the lover's leavings if only he could hold her, and feel her warm against him. As he stared into the darkness, what he wanted was to turn to her and take her in his arms, but he feared that if he did reach out, she would resist his touch. He had, he thought, never really touched her. Their bodies had bumped together, like those of strangers in a crowd who are thrust into physical intimacy by the pressure of the crowd's movement.

Henry listened to her breathing and wondered if she was asleep; he could not be sure. He wanted to ask her what was in her mind, what thoughts of her lover, what memories of how they had clung together, but it was wrong to ask, to intrude on the secret places of her love. It was not something he could share. He imagined the two of them standing inside a barn door, their bodies held tightly together in the moment before they must separate, the horses and cattle snuffling and breathing in the darkness behind them.

Perhaps she carried her lover's seed inside her. Perhaps she would bear his child. At that moment Henry felt that he didn't care, anything so long as she didn't abandon him. Whatever else, he loved her. When he stood in the pulpit and, looking over the congregation, caught a glimpse of her face, the words would tangle in his mind, and God would vanish. He would look away from her, to the worn face of an old man who had spent his life on the land, and in his sight, Henry would once again know himself as the young parson and would remember the sermon he had prepared.

Was this love or only a form of idolatry? Perhaps he would never know. She had become a part of him before he was formed, like a nail driven into a young tree and left so that the tree grows round it and incorporates the nail inside its flesh. She had grown into him, into his flesh. He could not know laughter or tears unless she was a part of them.

From time to time, he saw his situation in the eyes of others, the cuckolded husband, the comic figure who hadn't the masculine vigour to control his wife. The preacher who had no right to give advice to others because of the disorder at the heart of his own life. He was to conduct a wedding service the next day. How could he do it?

How many of his parishioners knew? He saw no sign that they were laughing at him, but they always kept a distance. It was one of the costs of being ordained that it was impossible to ever be treated quite like another human being. It was like bearing a plague.

If they knew, what would they advise? That he send her away? Would he have any career in the church without her? These worldly concerns drew him away from her, from the sense of the electric body that lay near him, gave him a momentary detachment. Perhaps now he could pray. For what? It was possible to pray for wisdom without knowing what that wisdom might be. He tried to find words to pray, and the prayer seemed to move with the rhythm of his wife's breathing, and he moved towards sleep.

Dreaming is too close. There is no space around the presences or the events. It is an imprisonment in the narrow ways of the brain. Wherever he looks, they are closer to him, watching, and he can't decide where it is safe. The others are all moving, but he stands perfectly still and waits for what is coming. He thinks perhaps he is going to be asked to preach, but he is aware that those around him are unbelievers, even diabolists, and he can't find the words that would be suitable. Then there is music and the crowd begins to move in a dance that is awkward and sensual. They are all men, and the dance they perform is the dance of the incubi. The words are repetitive and ridiculous: *Demons are a girl's best friend*, they sing. Amelia is with them; they are going to possess her, to use her. Henry wants to tell Amelia that he will wait for her when they are finished and she is hurt and frightened, but she won't listen. Then she is gone, and the incubi are delivering a lecture to Henry telling him that this is the first page of the

Book of Acts. Everything that happens is part of the Book of Acts.

Henry knows it is dangerous to try to escape from the incubi, but he forces himself to turn his back and run; of course it is a dream, and he can't move.

Norman knew they were coming to get him. He'd seen them shining their lights. Ever since, he'd been curled tight in his corner, trying to be quiet so they wouldn't even hear his breathing, but his breathing was loud; he was sweating and his body was stiff. He was sure that they were all getting together, the Holey Ghost and Thy Spirit and the Dark Angels because they'd found out what Norman had done to the white cat. He didn't go meaning to hurt the cat, but when Glory was gone, and they said she wasn't coming back, Norman thought he'd take the cat with him and keep it. But the cat ran away and when Norman chased it, it hid in the closet and wouldn't come out. All he could think of was how Glory had gone away from him, and now the cat wouldn't come, and he went in the closet and grabbed the cat, but when he grabbed it, the cat scratched him, and then he was so mad he was shouting, and the only thing he could do was kill the cat, Glory's white cat, and when it was dead, he threw it down on the floor and ran away to hide.

What she needed, Rose decided, was some form of spiritual exercises, calisthenics for the soul. Whatever was within her was sluggish, close enough to inert. She had let the bishop be the source of her spiritual energy, and now he was passive and silent, she too was slack and slow. She could still manage a certain amount of anger, faced with fools like Edgar Worral, but anger wasn't enough. It left no resonance.

She sat at her drawing board, doodling, realized that she had been drawing coffins and little crosses. Her mind had entered the graveyard shift. She had made her choices in life, and she had ended up alone. Well that was her choice, or her many choices, one small one after another, no one seeming of much consequence, but the end of it was the woman who sat here doodling coffins. It had been all right while the bishop was well, but now she was alone again. She doodled a woman's face, tried to make it look like Joanne. Which Joanne? The one she had known in the past, the one who had opened the world to her, through whose eyes she had seen things new, or the placid maternal figure she visited from time to time, to whom she had nothing to say? To whom she had nothing to say because that was what Joanne had willed.

It came; it passed. There was a space between them where before there had been a vivid electrical awareness. Rose would find herself observing her friend, cold, suspicious, detached. If she saw Joanne coming out of a classroom, talking to someone, smiling, her body would go chill and stiff. She would turn away, not to be seen. She didn't want Joanne to know the blank murderous eyes that spied on her. Then would come the temptation to follow the two of them, Joanne and whoever else it might be, dodging along the hall, driven and humiliated, until the huge relief of the moment when Joanne parted from the person who walked beside her and the association was proved temporary, inconsequential.

Yet Rose would be compelled to bring up the name, later, when she and Joanne were together, to bring it up, in passing, but watching her friend's face for some slight alteration in the light that flickered in the blue eyes.

Increasingly, there was a kind of madness in Rose because she knew Joanne was moving away from her, but they couldn't speak of it, and Rose was haunted by the need to do something decisive, though she couldn't imagine what that might be.

It came; it is passing. Rose is losing something she could never name. Joanne is not as close to her now. There is a man who shares her music.

Rose sees Joanne's face turn towards her, the small features caught in the light, and she tries to read the expression. The man stands behind, his finger on the paper, his eyes down, and he ignores Rose's presence at the doorway. But Joanne has looked towards her, and Rose studies the expression with the care she might give to a difficult parable, but no matter how she studies the expression, she can find nothing final in it, nothing certain. Joanne's face is calm enough, and yet not settled, somewhere between two things, and neither one has a name. The mouth is on the point of opening to speak and yet it does not. The eyes are neither warm nor cold.

Rose is angered that the man will not acknowledge her presence; he only waits for Joanne to return her concentration to the music that he is explaining to her. Rose cannot understand music; she has the voice of a starling or a grackle. These two sing duets together in church, and Rose tries to shut her ears to the way the voices blend, and the bodies seem to move in concert, even though they are several feet apart.

Joanne's eyes are holding hers, and Rose cannot, no matter how she looks, understand the tentative expression that the face holds. His face is shut, complacent. He is impatient for Rose to leave, for Joanne to turn her gaze back down to the page of music, where his finger indicates some point of harmony that Rose's blunt ear could never hear. His hand rests on the back of the chair, a rather thick hand that rests only a few inches from Joanne's shoulder. He is posed and his body will not move to acknowledge Rose's presence. His other hand, the one that is on the music, is only a few inches from Joanne's, and the two hands seem part of some other moment, not the one where Rose's eyes and Joanne's meet across the space of the room. If Rose could speak, she might be able to force this moment to some definition, victory or defeat, something that could be put in words, but Rose can't make, in her grackle's croak, a single sound, and so the nebulous intensity will never take on any precise shape. It will only have the shape of what came after, as Rose stood at the saw and pushed the piece of wood across the blade, thinking that the scream of the saw was the only music she understood, and then the scream was her scream and there was blood everywhere and she had the stump of her finger wrapped in the end of her blouse and was running across the school yard towards the hospital half a block away. Ever after that day, Rose tried to remember what was before the blood, to understand what had happened. Sometimes she thought she had noticed the saw approaching her finger and had felt that the loss was a kind of sacrifice, something to match with the grackle voice and heavy legs that marked her as untouchable, a solitary soul who would no longer be troubled by cool, incomprehensible looks.

Her father lectured her and phoned the woodworking teacher, Mr. Bosk, and bawled him out for letting Rose use the Carpentry shop at night, and Rose had to go one afternoon and try to apologize and then Mr. Bosk, who had always treated her as special, lectured her, saying he thought he'd taught her better than that, and Rose had to explain that she was tired that night and shouldn't have come, and he took back the key he'd given her and said he regretted it, but he had no choice, the principal had been after him. So the little hanging shelf that Rose was making for Joanne would never be finished. She became a kind of celebrity in school, and grotesque stories were told about the amount of blood that she had shed on the floor of the woodworking shop, and what she had said when she reached the hospital. She became a fictional character, and she was not altogether unhappy with this.

In the school hall, Rose would pass a group of boys.

"Keep it in your pants," Tim Wahl would say, "or Rose will cut it off."

Blair Runions, the joker — his inveterate jokes the

natural result, perhaps, of being called Blair Onions for so many years – had invented a story, which he embellished with more and more inventive detail, telling how as Rose went screaming off to the hospital, the end of her finger had begun hopping around the woodworking room like some kind of tiny elf, trying to find the finger it belonged to.

"Watch out," Bruce Feuer would shout through the doorway of the boy's washroom, "here comes Rose with her saw."

Rose understood these consequences of the accident and in them she found a kind of safety, but she would never be sure whether she had been aware of the saw approaching the finger or whether that was something she added, a kind of nightmare image that overlay the reality and became part of it, and just as she could never understand that, she could never know quite what she had seen on Joanne's face. Once she believed that what she saw was an invitation, to speak, to interrupt and become part of that small scene at the table, the black piano in the background, the coffee cups set aside, the light catching their edges. Perhaps Joanne had wished her to speak. Another time, the look would ask Rose why she was there, interrupting, interfering. The man had kept his eyes harshly averted, making Rose, the intruder, unreal, a thing of wood that could be cut to pieces without blood or pain. With the saw that took off her finger, she proved that she had blood, that she was made of flesh, but having once sacrificed that finger, she was forever safe. She had concentrated her pain in that moment, defined her position as an eccentric so that from that day on she could act as she pleased. She was, from that moment, no longer young, and the responses of the young weren't expected from her. She was, from that moment, an ageless thing of wood, her passions those of a puppet, harmless and predictable; she was free of love, free, at least, of love that might become intoxication, madness, left with the love — of her parents, of God — that left no wreckage in its wake. She had gone to work in her father's office, and by the time of his death, she was running the insurance agency, but once he was dead, it seemed to have no point, and she sold the agency and left town. For a while she had worked for a church mission, and she had used her free time in what were thought eccentric ways; reading odd books and woodworking. She had stood as godmother to Joanne's baby, and was pleased and proud; she liked the man Joanne had eventually married. The madness was gone, like a fever that flares and vanishes.

Henry woke to the sound of the explosion, waited for the plaster to fall, then gradually, as his eyes took in the shapes of what was around him, became aware that he was in his own room, and old, and that it was raining outside. It was thunder that had wakened him, but he had believed that he was back in London during the blitz, on that long night in the spring of 1941 when the two of them had met.

How easily that meeting might never have happened; if either one had changed his movements by a few feet, a minute's time, they might have passed by in the blacked-out streets, neither knowing that the other was there.

Henry had come up to London on leave from the camp in Sussex. He knew no one in London, and he had spent the afternoon in Kew Gardens, enjoying the quiet, the sense of calm and civility. For a long time, he simply stared out over the mud flats of the Thames at low tide. And in the calm of that afternoon, he thought he might have recovered something almost lost, some sense of what existed within and beyond the man who looked and the world he saw. He had read a few lines of George Herbert, less for the meaning of the lines than to hear the gentle sureness of the voice. It was hearing the voice of a friend. Sometimes when he read Paul's Epistles, he could hear the voice with the same sense of closeness and comfort, but not now; the apostle's voice was too powerful, too demanding. Henry needed something gentle.

It was a curious thing, being an army chaplain. For the parish minister, the daily and weekly round was so traditional, so much anchored in the quotidian patterns of the lives of ordinary people, that his work became almost invisible. But among the men of an army, there was no pattern, at least of that sort; the life had patterns enough, rigid, many of them, hours of rising, hours of military exercises, hours of meals, but the structure was unnatural. Nothing in the life was rich, nothing had the rhythm of tradition. The men sought women, persistently, frantically, but the women could never be a part of their lives. There were no shared children. Henry had never before understood so clearly how much of human life is shaped by the presence of children. Men and women come together, and children are born, and then life takes its shape around the helpless little ones. The army was there to defend that life, to defend those children, but it did it by creating an unnatural world in which young men were isolated from all the things that would normally have given their lives meaning – work, love, a vision of the future. For these young men, the future was hypothetical. If they survived, only then would they have a life to live.

Sometimes Henry thought that he belonged in the army camp because he had no children, no little ones to give his existence meaning. When some young man came to tell him that he had impregnated an English girl and was faced with the consequences, Henry often wished to cry out that he envied the young man the very thing that oppressed him, that he had made a child. Because Henry was older than most of the soldiers – old enough that he feared he would be left in England when the time for battle finally came – they expected fatherly advice from him, and too often, he felt unable to give it. All around was the laughter of his ghosts.

The trip to London was an attempt to reach into himself and find the strength to go on playing his unnatural role in that unnatural world. So he sat in Kew Gardens and he read George Herbert and felt some kind of continuity between the English tradition that surrounded him, and the words of the liturgy that had penetrated his boyhood and made him Christ's servant, however inadequately.

Any moment of that day might have been different, might have prevented the meeting. If the weather had stayed cool, Henry would not have sat as long at the gardens, but the sun shone all day long, and the daffodils with their pale tissue of yellow blossom shone with it. If Henry had not stopped at the tea shop opposite the gardens, if he had not caught the train that pulled into the station just as he arrived but had waited for the next, they would not have met.

The night streets were haunted with darkness during the black-out. The figure of a warden on his bicycle would appear a few feet away and vanish almost immediately. Voices were disembodied. The warden's bicycle tires would hum off into the void and there would be an exchange with some unseen figure, a few words about the weather or the chance of bombs falling that night, and then, as if the enemy planes had been called up by the words, the sirens started to wail. Doors opened and people moved through the dark streets towards the shelters. One sound would catch the ear and then another from some other direction, closer or farther off. The cry of the sirens rose and fell, and there was a constant undertone to all the sounds, an undertone that Henry finally realized was the sound of approaching German bombers. He could follow the crowd and find a shelter, but he didn't want to do that. He wanted to stay above ground and challenge death. Perhaps find an open pub and sit among ordinary people who waited fatalistically as the explosives fell. Henry had always been thankful that Anglican ministers were not expected to be teetotallers, like the ministers of those protestant denominations who refused to use real wine for communion and replaced it with grape juice, and since he was surrounded by men who drank whenever they could lay their hands on alcohol, he found he was drinking more often than he had at home; it was both a pleasure and good tactics to join his men in the pub. He learned more about them there than he ever would by preaching over them. And a little to drink was a pleasant habit.

He turned a corner in the darkness, and somewhere in the distance, he heard the drumbeat of the first explosions. Ahead of him, he heard a door open and a man's voice.

"Watch it, mate. You near knocked me down."

Figures moved, footsteps vanished into the dark street, and as Henry came up to the doorway, he could just make out the sign of a pub. He thought he could hear voices inside, and he found the door, as much by touch as by sight, and opened it. He could see light around the black-out curtain, and he pushed through to where a small group of people stood by a bar, and two or three others sat at small tables. Henry felt, suddenly, out of place, and as if he should never have left his hotel to wander through the dark streets, looking for something that would never be found. He thought he might turn and leave, as if he had come in by mistake, but the eye of the publican, a tall red-faced man with a shiny bald pate, was on him, so he walked towards the bar. From the other end, a figure in khaki rose to leave, and it was just as he turned to the door that Henry saw his face, and when he saw it, he shook with a chill that nearly paralyzed him.

Here, where death came across the sky towards them, where men and women waited for destruction to fall like rain, they had met. Call it Providence or chance or synchronicity, Henry saw before him the man he had wanted to meet, had wanted not to meet, until the two contradictory desires were the same.

"Wilf."

At the moment he spoke the man's name, they had already seen each other, been recognized, walked to the edge of the world and paused there, in the middle of the random slaughter that buzzed its alarm across the sky. They stood silent, patient, as if they had both waited forever for this meeting, but now it had happened, and freed from expectation, both were stilled. As if by agreement, they walked up to the bar and ordered.

There was an explosion, somewhere not far away, and the glasses over the bar rattled.

"D'you think Jerry's got your name on one of those, Clyde?" one of the customers said to the red-faced man behind the bar. The publican only shrugged. Henry and the soldier sat in silence, both in uniform, two men who had come to a strange country for war. All over the world, men were coming together to kill one another.

"I'm for home," a woman said and walked to the door. As she opened it, the sound of sirens and the hum of bomber engines grew louder and then muted again. Henry searched for words, but found none. Perhaps even here at the edge of death, they had nothing to say.

He turned and looked at the younger man and felt,

momentarily, that Amelia was there in the room with them. That was why he had wanted to meet the man. He believed that Amelia's lover must carry her lost presence with him.

Wilf was staring into his whisky. He picked it up and threw it back, then turned to Henry.

"How is your wife?" he asked.

Of course. Wilf didn't know. The bombers approached, the noise of their engines louder. Henry found it hard to articulate words, took a drink before he did.

"Amelia's dead."

The presence that had come close to him came closer, glowed brighter; she was there, vivid and hurt, in both minds and somehow in the air between them. Wilf lifted his glass to the man behind the bar who poured a whisky which he drank off. He reached out his glass for another, drank it and put money on the bar.

"Let's get out of here," he said.

Henry finished his drink and followed the other man to the door; they passed through the black-out curtains to the outside, where the air was full of noise and flashes of light. The searchlights were playing over the sky; anti-aircraft guns went off with their regular-irregular rhythm; there was flame in the air somewhere in the distance, bombs intervened, their detonation coming with an unpredictable suddenness.

"How?" Wilf asked. "How did she die?"

His voice was so close, so intimate against the background of sirens and explosions. Henry saw incendiaries coming down through the air like vicious stars, and he realized that he could smell burning.

"We were in the Arctic," he said. "She walked away from the mission one day while I was out. It was the beginning of winter. I looked for her for two days, but I never found her."

A figure appeared beside them and turned on them a small light with a blue hood. It was a woman in dungarees and a metal helmet, with large pouches hanging from her belt. She had a jowly, suspicious face.

"Not safe here you know. You'd best go to the shelter. Just along the road a bit."

"We'll be all right," Wilf said. "He has God on his side."

The woman looked huffy.

"Bad enough those who have to be out being out," she said. "Never say I didn't warn you."

A bomb fell close enough that they felt the street shake beneath their feet.

"You see," she said, triumphantly, as she mounted her bicycle and vanished into the darkness.

They were left alone again. There was flame closer now, and they could hear men shouting and there was an orange light visible between the piles of ruins beside them.

"You let her go?" Wilf asked. "You just let her walk away and die?"

"I told you, I looked for two days."

"Why not three? Why not five?"

"There was a snowstorm. It wasn't possible."

Henry was disturbed by the false sound in his words. What Wilf was saying to him was what he had said over and over in his own mind. The answers sounded rehearsed because he had spoken them a hundred times to the accuser in his own heart.

"Did you know about us?" he asked.

"Yes. Of course."

"Why didn't you do anything?"

Henry opened his mouth to explain, couldn't, couldn't speak, couldn't breathe. He began to walk, away, anywhere, down a passage between two buildings, a passage with only a dim light at the end. The noise seemed to be increasing, as if it was trapped in this narrow channel like a wind seeking an outlet. A flare burst in the sky, and everything was alight, but unreal. He didn't look back to see if Wilf was following, only plunged on through the passage. The pavement was cobblestone, and he was aware of its bumpy surface, even through his heavy army boots; that seemed strange, but when he tried to think about it, he could only measure over and over the slight rolling of his boots as he walked. There was an explosion so close that the whole earth shook, and in a reflex of self-defense, Henry pushed his back against one of the buildings. Another explosion followed. His ears were deafened and the force of the blast pressed him against the wall where he stood. For a minute or more, there seemed to be no sound around him, only a soft roaring inside his head, but then gradually the sirens and the demented buzzing of the bombers penetrated his ears. He went on along the passage, as if it meant something to reach the end, and when he did, he saw, across the road, the ruins of a building that had just been hit. A gas pipe was burning, and the light of the burning gas added to the weird light from the flares. Two floors up, hanging in the air as if suspended there, was a single room with no walls. In it sat a bathtub. Henry crossed the road and stared at the ruins, and as he did, heard a knocking sound that seemed to come from somewhere beneath the rubble of stone and wood, then a voice calling weakly, "Help me, I'm alive, help me."

Henry went to the place where he'd heard the voice.

"I'll try to dig you out," he said. As he began to lift pieces of the bombed building away, he found that Wilf was beside him. They worked without speaking.

"Are you still all right?" Henry would say as they worked. "We're getting closer." And the voice would reply. The woman in helmet and dungarees was beside them again.

"Is that you, Missus Goodridge?" the woman shouted down into the ruins.

"Yes."

"Are? You? Hurt?"

She spoke slowly and loudly as if using a loud hailer over a vast distance. She had a pad and pencil in her hand.

"My leg. It's trapped."

"This is Bessie, luv. The warden. I'll make my report and fetch a rescue party and an ambulance."

She vanished. There was an opening through the rubble now, but it was too small to climb through. Henry put his face against it.

"Mrs Goodridge?"

"Yes?" She sounded like a schoolgirl.

"We're getting close now."

"Bless you," the voice said.

Henry stood up. Wilf was staring at the rubble. It was darker now, and harder to see.

"If we're not careful," Wilf said, "we'll bring that down on her."

A staircase, with a wall hanging over it, was suspended above the pile of wood and plaster that they were heaving aside. It was impossible to see what was supporting it.

"If we can work backwards," Henry said, "maybe we can make the hole bigger without moving that. Then one of us can get inside." He began to drag away material from the small hole they'd made. There was a sudden shift and his leg went down as a pile of plaster dropped into the basement. Henry caught a wooden joist and kept himself from falling through. Wilf gave him his hand and pulled him back out. There was a large hole open to the basement where the woman was trapped.

"We need a light," Wilf said.

"The warden will send someone."

"We don't dare try to move her in the dark. We could bring it all down."

"I'll go down and stay with her, until they come with a light."

"How are you going to get down?"

Henry searched through the ruins and found a long piece of wooden joist. He put it down the hole until he touched something solid, then set it at a slope, leaning against a stable piece of the floor.

"You hold that steady," he said, "and I'll slide down till I find solid footing."

Wilf planted his feet and took hold of the joist. Henry dropped his feet down the edge of the hole, locked his legs and arms round the joist and began to slide down. The piece of wood was too narrow to support him comfortably, and it dug into his body, but he moved along, kicking one foot down to find the floor. At last he felt it beneath him. He could see nothing.

"Where are you?" he asked.

"Here," said the voice from somewhere in front of him. Henry was afraid he might step on her so he bent in a low crouch and moved with his hands in front of him, until he felt himself touch her.

"There," he said. "I've found you. We can't get you out without a light, but I'll stay with you until they get here."

"Bless you," she said again. There was a pause as she gathered her breath. "Who are you?" she asked.

"My name's Henry Wade. I'm a chaplain with the Canadian Army."

"What are you doing here?"

"I was passing by when I heard you. I'm on leave in London."

The sounds of the air raid went on and yet what Henry could hear most clearly was her laboured breathing. The basement was full of dust and smoke.

"I was never much for church, I'm afraid. Couldn't see much in it really."

"Perhaps you're just not ready yet. Sometimes when you're older, it starts to make more sense."

"My grandmother was chapel."

"We're all of us trying to get to the same place."

Again they waited. Henry could hear plaster trickling down the walls, as if the load of rubble above was slowly moving, perhaps preparing to fall.

"I think I'm going to die," the young woman said.

"They'll be here soon. Would you like me to hold your hand?"

"Yes."

He found her hand and held it in his own. She was moaning softly, and he didn't like the wet sound of her breathing. He looked back up through the hole, hoping to see a rescue party arrive, but there was only a flickering of unnatural light against the ruins.

"There was a hymn," she said, "we sang in school."

"What was it about?"

"I can't rightly remember. It was the tune I was fond of."

"Would you like me to pray?"

"No," she said. "Just hold my hand."

The buzzing of the airplanes rose and fell in waves. Another bomb fell in the district, and plaster dribbled more heavily on top of them. If the rubble came down, they might both be killed. He began to feel angry that the rescue party hadn't come, that the warden was taking forever to get them here, and he looked up once more towards the hole, but no one appeared.

He couldn't hear her breathing. He bent towards the face, but he could hear no sound. He put his fingers against her lips, and they were open and flaccid. She was unconscious or dead. He laid his hand against her face, as if the life of his body might flow into hers. He waited.

In a few more minutes, the rescue party arrived with a ladder and lights. The girl was dead. Henry made a short silent prayer and left the men in helmets, with their kind, brutal efficiency, to get her body out. He climbed their ladder and made his way back to the street. Wilf was sitting there on a pile of rubble, smoking.

"I thought you'd be gone," Henry said.

"I waited for you."

"Why?"

"Let's go somewhere where we can talk."

"My hotel isn't far from here."

The two men set off down the street, side by side. They passed bomb sites from earlier raids, which now looked passive, ancient, the scars of forgotten wounds. Around them, the noise of planes, guns, bombs went on and on until it seemed to be occurring inside the skull. The sky, lit by distant fires, was a dark mud and the search lights slithered over it.

"Do you still believe in God?" Wilf said.

I believe in God the Father Almighty Maker of Heaven and Earth and in Jesus Christ his only Son . . .

"Yes."

"Where was your God when the bomb fell on that building and that girl was trapped? Was that His idea of fun? Where was He when she was dying?"

"He was in you and me, doing what we could to help, in her being brave and honest."

"That's not God."

"What is it?"

"Human decency. You don't need God to explain it."

They walked on, and though there was light in the sky, the streets seemed sunk into the black-out; Henry had to struggle to find his way, but finally he led them into the small private hotel where he had rented a room. It seemed empty; everyone had gone to the nearest shelter. There was only one dim bulb burning in the hall. Henry led the way up the stairs to his room. The room was dark and the curtains were open, and across the city, he could see a huge fire, orange flames rolling into the sky, dancing and retiring and leaping up again. To each side were lesser fires where smaller flames danced in the air. Fire was magic; it was impossible not to be moved by its beauty.

"Is that what hell will be like?" Wilf said, closing the door behind him.

Henry didn't turn and look at him. Words came from somewhere in the past.

"Hell hath no limit, nor is circumscrib'd
In one self place. . . . When all the world dissolves,
And every creature shall be purified,
All places shall be hell that are not heaven."

"Who wrote that?"

"Christopher Marlowe. They called him an atheist."

"He sounds Christian to me. Gloating over damnation."

"I'm not very interested in hell," Henry said, "but I think what he means is that we carry hell and heaven inside us, and at every moment we're choosing one or the other."

Wilf sat down in a chair in the corner.

"Last night," Wilf said, "when I got to London on the train, I thought I was going to find her here."

"Amelia?"

"I was sure that she was somewhere in London, and I spent half the night walking the streets. I was crazy. I couldn't see anything in the black-out. I'd never have seen her if she was there. But I could feel it, that she was just around the next corner. This afternoon I started again, walking the streets, staring at the faces."

"And you found me."

"You knew about us. I never realized."

"At first I only knew that there was someone. I didn't know who it was. Then one day, I met you on the street, and the way you looked at me made me sure it was you."

"Why did you put up with it?"

"Because I loved her. I wanted her to be happy. That sounds simple, but it never was. Every second was a struggle, and my mind was always in a tangle, trying to work through it."

"Weren't you jealous?"

"I sometimes thought I'd die of it."

"Did you tell her?"

"No. I tried to pretend it didn't exist. I was frightened too, that she'd leave me. I couldn't imagine living without her, what I'd be or do. And if she asked for a divorce, I'd have to leave the ministry. I loved her so much. When she came back from being with you, I wanted to cry, because I was so relieved to see her. After a while, the jealousy didn't seem to matter much. I could put it away somewhere or I could just give it to God. So long as she stayed with me, it would be all right."

A new and higher burst of flame, shining and golden, rose from the site of one of the fires.

"When I came back from the West," Wilf said, "I went to the parsonage. I decided on the train that I was going to walk up to the door and ask her to come away with me. I got off the train, and as I walked up the street, it was a grey kind of a day, there was a little rain falling, and I imagined how the two of us would walk back down the street together to get on the train and never come back. I started to run, but when I was close to the house, I stopped and tried to make myself be sensible, but still I'd keep walking faster; I couldn't help it. I was even ready to meet you if you came to the door. I was going to hold my head up high and ask to see Amelia. But when a complete stranger came to the door, I couldn't talk. I had my words all ready, but nothing would come out. I think she figured I was some kind of a tramp looking for a handout. Finally I managed to ask for Amelia, and she said you'd both gone away, somewhere up north. I said something foolish and went away, and I just wandered. Went back to where my father's farm used to be, and I ended up lying on the ground in the woods, under a little rock outcropping where I was sheltered from the rain. It was cold, but I fell asleep. When I woke up it was almost dark and I was shivering so hard I couldn't stop. I got up and I ran all the way to the station and took the train back out west."

"Why did you go away in the first place?"

"Stupid. Just stupid. I was young, and I was scared of the whole thing. Me and the minister's wife. But I was pretty proud of myself, too. Then I got the chance of a job selling newspaper subscriptions, travelling around. It was the first offer I'd had of a job for months, and I couldn't turn it down. I got travelling from town to town with these guys. You'd knock on doors, and sometimes the woman would be home alone, and she'd give you a coffee. We all made jokes about it. I started to think it wasn't anything so special, with Amelia. Once I'd been away two weeks, and when I came back, and I saw her, she cried so hard I was scared."

"So you ran away."

"And when I came back, it was too late."

"Did you love her?"

"I guess I did. I do now."

"So do I."

"Does her no God-damn good."

"Maybe not."

As he looked towards the great fires to the east, Henry saw dust and rubble rise where a new bomb had fallen. Men and women were dying out there in the night.

"I knew something was wrong after you left," Henry said, "even before I heard you were gone. She looked half-dead, or she'd go out in public and be so cheerful that the church women would be shocked. A minister's wife is supposed to smile, but not too much. People were beginning to criticize her, and it made me hate them. I started trying to get assigned to an arctic mission. When I told her, I thought she might refuse to come with me, but she just asked when we'd be leaving."

"I wonder which one of us she was running away from when she went out to get lost and die."

"Both, I suppose. An Eskimo shaman told me she was tired and wanted to go to the Moon Spirit. The Eskimos have no taboo against suicide."

"How long were you up there?"

"We'd been there just over a year when she disappeared. It was another year before a boat came in and I could leave. Sometimes I believed that when I got back south, I'd hear that she'd been seen, that somehow you'd come to the Arctic to get her. It was impossible, but alone up there my mind hardly knew what was possible or impossible. Tonight in that pub, I felt as if she was there because we were both there."

There was a silence in the room, a silence surrounded by the rage of war outside. Henry tried to find her presence in the silence, but it was gone.

"I never really understood what was wrong between us," Henry said. "When we met, loving her was something that had always been inevitable, but I suppose it's like that for everyone. You're young and lonely, and suddenly there's someone who seems to be everything you've wanted, someone who's as close to you as your own skin. They come to me when they're planning to get married, and they all look the same. In love, they say, and they're not wrong. They're in it, they're drowned in it, and they're so beautiful. I say sensible things to them, about the difficulties of marriage, but they never pay any attention, and probably they shouldn't. Perhaps in ten years, in some dark moment when they regret the whole thing, they'll remember something I've said, and it will help them through. Or maybe they'll be among the lucky ones, and somehow it will work out. Marriage isn't there for men and women, really. It's there for children."

"Why didn't you have children?"

"She was afraid, somehow. I thought the time would come when it would be right, but it never did."

In front of him the city went on burning. Lights crossed the sky, looking for the planes. Henry couldn't turn to look at the man behind him. But he had to ask.

"Did she want to have children with you?" Henry asked. He had to know.

"She talked about it." The harpoon entered the flesh.

"And that frightened you too."

"Yes."

"Tell me about it. How you met her. What happened?"

"Are you sure you want to know?"

"Yes."

"I was fishing in the mill-pond one day when she came by. The path came right close to where I was standing, so I had to move to let her past. I said something, I don't remember what, and we started talking. Since I came back to town, there was no one much for me to talk to. My father, after he lost the farm, just sat and stared at the wall. I had no job. I got talking to her, and somehow that made her talk too. Then I caught a fish, and we both got excited about that. And then it seemed dangerous all of a sudden. It was so natural, the way we laughed together, that I think we were both scared. She started to leave, but she asked me if I fished there often, and I said I did, there was nothing else to do and a meal of fish saved money. She walked away, and I watched her, the way she walked. That night, late, when I thought everybody was in bed, I went past your house — she told me who she was, who you were — and I stood there in the dark and thought about her sleeping inside, with you. I didn't really know you, but I never had much use for religion. My mother got religion for a while, and it was pretty bad. I thought Amelia was too good to be a minister's wife. I went home and I decided I'd spend a lot of time fishing at the mill-pond, in case she came back. Later on, she told me she was looking out the window that night. I couldn't see her, but she was watching me where I stood in the road there. A couple of days later, I was fishing again, and I saw her along the river, below the dam. She'd been wearing a straw hat, but she'd taken it off and she was carrying it in her hand. She was pretending not to look up where I was, and I looked away and didn't watch her coming, so when she came up the path, we both acted as if we hadn't seen each other. I don't know why."

He stopped. The picture was vivid in Henry's mind; he remembered the straw hat, how he loved the way she looked in it. He stared across the night city. The biggest of the fires had burned down, but another had started to the north of it. Henry could see the dark shape of a church steeple in silhouette in front of it.

"Do you want to hear all this?" Wilf asked.

"Yes."

"Why?"

"Because it makes me feel closer to her."

"Doesn't it hurt?"

"Of course. But tell me."

"When she came up the path, she had a flower in her hand, one of those dark blue flags that grow wild beside the river. She gave it to me. I didn't know what to do. I didn't have a lot of experience with women, and here was the Anglican minister's wife, who was older than I was, and beautiful, and she was handing me a flower. We talked some more that day, and we met another time, and then we started to arrange to meet."

The view of the night city was blurred now, and Henry reached up to wipe the tears from his face.

"Were you good to her?" he asked. "Did you make her happy?"

"Something made her happy," Wilf said. "I don't know if it was me. Was I good to her? She said I was. I'd never met anyone like her. I'd had a couple of other girls, but they were like meat and potatoes, ordinary, you knew where you were at. They wouldn't have given me a flower; they would have waited for me to give them one. I knew Amelia was something special, but I didn't know what it all meant, and it made me want to run."

Henry listened, silent. He thought that perhaps he had turned to stone, that if a bomb fell on this building, his body would not bleed, but shatter like a piece of marble sculpture, shatter and fall into dust.

"Who was Percy Nash?" Wilf asked.

"What?"

"Did you know someone named Percy Nash?"

"I knew who he was. Why?"

"Amelia once said that she thought this Percy Nash was her father. She was crying. She'd start to cry sometimes just out of nowhere. You know what she was like, I guess."

"I never saw her cry."

"No?"

"No."

"She was talking about you, and she said that she was the wrong person for you to have married, that she was a bad person, like Percy Nash. I asked her who he was, but she wouldn't tell me, except she thought that he was her real father. That her mother used to talk about him."

"Percy Nash lived in the town we came from. He was hanged for murder. My father was the lawyer who defended him."

"Could he have been her father?"

"I don't think so. There was a lot of bad gossip about Percy but I never heard that."

"Sometimes she'd cry and then laugh it off, but that night she couldn't stop. I tried to comfort her, but it seemed as if I'd got in over my head. I didn't know what to do or say."

"Why could she tell you things and not me?"

"You were too perfect. And I don't think she liked religion much. She laughed a lot when I made fun of it. She said the people in the church were cruel."

"Some of them probably were. When we were leaving to go to the Arctic, one of the men took me aside and told me that he'd seen you and Amelia together. He thought I should know. It was when we were leaving he told me, when it was obviously all over. It was pure malice."

"Christians are great ones for that."

"Not just Christians. They have no patent on malice."

"I'm not so sure. Once you start thinking of yourself as a good person."

"Maybe."

"How did you do it? When you knew about me and Amelia, how did you just keep quiet and accept it?"

"I don't know what you think religion is, but for me it's a door in a small room. We live in that room, and things close in on us and they hurt us, and we see ourselves being weak and worse than weak. But if there's a door in the room, it's different. You know that there's something outside, and that gives you freedom and strength. I try to keep looking for the door. If you think about what Jesus said, that's what He's talking about, how you find the door and open it."

"Didn't you ever get trapped in that little room so you felt you had to smash your way out?"

"I got angry, mostly with myself, because I didn't know how to reach her. I was failing her, and I didn't know what was wrong. Maybe I thought that being alone in the Arctic would be some kind of solution because we'd be so isolated. But it killed her."

"It didn't kill you."

"No."

"You were stronger, and you won."

"I don't believe that."

"Marriage is like that. I watched my old man and my old lady. It was war, just like this one. Night raids, dogfights, sneak attacks."

"I don't know why Amelia loved you, when you're such a cynic."

"It was a relief. It made her laugh. A human being can only stand so much holiness."

There was something in his voice that began to rouse Henry's anger, something confident and unquestioning, hard. It hurt to think that Amelia had offered herself to this man, had told him things she couldn't tell Henry. She had betrayed his love; his entire, foolish, self-abnegating love had been nothing in the eyes which had found beauty in this cynical young man who was prepared to leave her as easily as he had taken her. Henry was filled with hatred, despising himself for telling this man things that he had never told another man or woman.

"Anyway," Wilf said, "she's dead. . . It doesn't feel like she's dead. I figured you'd settled down somewhere, that she had two or three kids, and if she saw me, she'd give a sentimental thought to the old days and go back to cooking dinner."

"No," Henry said. "You prevented that from happening. You took that future away from her, and then you denied her."

"She was alive last night. Alive for me. She was alive and right here in London. When I was walking around the streets, I nearly shouted her name."

"It's easy to be romantic about her when she's gone. You failed her when she was there in front of you."

Wilf didn't answer. Since they had come into the

room, neither one had changed position. Wilf sat in the chair by the bed, and Henry stood by the window and stared across the evil carnival of the bombed city, all its lights and noise, standing away from it all, a spectator who might, with a slight variation in the course of one of the German bombers become, in a second, a victim. The fires that leaped and glittered and evoked some primordial awe and excitement were burning the homes of ordinary men and women, the businesses into which they had put their lives. Henry could not know them; he was isolated from their lives, shut up in this dark room where the two of them tried to justify their actions, to get some grip on the past.

If either of them moved, the magic would be destroyed, and they would be unable to speak; they would be strangers again, but so long as they stood here in the dark, not looking at one another, the words would come. Perhaps they were talking, not to each other at all, but to the lovely delicate woman they had touched or tried to touch. If they had both loved her, was it the same love, parcelled out between them? There was one whole and entire love, and what each of them had known was a part of that. And above that were all the larger ones, the love of truth, the love of God. Doors of the small room. Henry wasn't free of his anger, but something in him was awakening, something that had become dormant when he left the Arctic. He had abandoned Amelia, unable to understand, hopeless, forced to put the thought of her out of his mind, since he could never reach her. Now he knew more of the story, and if it was painful, still he was awake, the pain roused him.

"Tell me something else about her," Henry said. "Tell me something beautiful."

Wilf was silent. The buzzing of the bombers seemed closer now, as if they were passing by at a lower altitude to drop their bombs more accurately.

"She couldn't ever say your name," Wilf said. "Not that we talked about you much, but sometimes it would happen. She couldn't say your name. She always found some way around it."

"Is that something beautiful?"

"It's what I remembered."

"Where did you go? To be together."

"Any place we thought we wouldn't be seen. I found a way to get in the old mill building. No one ever came there. It had been abandoned for years. We could always hear the river."

From the parsonage window, it was almost possible to see the roof of the old mill, a little farther along the concession road, and in fact from the church roof, the top of the mill was just visible. Henry remembered catching a glimpse of it when he was on the church roof helping replace the old shingles. Perhaps as he looked that way, the two of them had been together in the dim light among the disused milling machines. And if Amelia had to mention him, she couldn't speak his name. Would that have made him too real, brought him too close to her? She wanted him not to be, so she took away his name. Amelia.

Amelia. Amelia. He spoke her name over and over in his mind.

"You're sure," Wilf asked, "that she must be dead? She couldn't have gone away somewhere."

"There was nowhere to go. There was a Hudson's Bay store, and the tents and the snow houses of the Eskimos. They moved all the time, depending on where the hunting was good. The day after she vanished, there was a terrible storm. No one could have lived through that."

"But you never found her body."

"No."

He never found her body. True in more senses than one, perhaps. It was a peculiar and specialized case of the problem of body and soul, this thing between men and women. Had he ever found Amelia's soul? No. Surely not. But how had he missed it? He had laboured to reach her. He had never found her soul, never found her body, though one terrible day he would see her skull.

He had expected too much, needed too much. He had expected her to be the mate of his soul, to be the gateway to some perfect freedom. From what he had seen, those marriages were best which settled into a friendship that, with time, became an intimate necessity. The ancients were right that erotic love was a madness; it was idolatry, the replacement of the absolute of God with one of his creatures.

All that might be true enough, but Henry would have given much — he didn't try to guess how much — simply to see her from time to time, to hear her laugh. Even if she couldn't speak his name.

"I'm going now," Wilf said. "I don't suppose we'll meet again. Or have anything to say if we do."

"I'm glad you told me the things you did. It's better to know."

"Not for me. I liked it better when I thought she was happy somewhere."

"Maybe she is."

"I don't believe in that nonsense. The dead are dead."

He walked out of the room, and Henry continued to stare across the torn city, where men and women were becoming whatever it is the dead become. A bomb fell, close enough that the glass in the window shook, and Henry wondered where Wilf was, if that bomb might have dropped where he walked through the dark streets. Would he, Henry wondered, be pleased if he heard that the man was dead?

Outside his window, the rain went on and on. Henry lay in his bed, old, silent, paralyzed. The dead are dead. Wilf was among them. Just over a year after their meeting, Henry had seen his name in the list of those killed at Dieppe.

Rose stood in the small empty room behind the cathedral and studied her drawings, trying to make sure that everything would work, that she hadn't made some foolish mistake in the original measurements or sketches. They all seemed right, though she was still uncertain whether to make the shelves permanent or adjustable. Perhaps she should look again to see how much variation there was in the size of the books. Yesterday afternoon, she'd suggested to Frank that some of the old books of vestry minutes from around the diocese might be kept here to make a little more room in the synod office. He was nervous about the whole idea, but she said she could put locks on some of the cupboards and they would be perfectly safe.

In fact, of course, the discussion had been mainly an excuse to let Frank know what she was doing and get it underway before she lost any more credit over Ishakak's presence in the bishop's apartment. For the time being he was still there, but only because of Rose's stubbornness, and she was beginning to wonder if she was doing her usual trick of being stubborn for the sheer pleasure of it.

She had managed to present the whole archive to Frank in a way that prevented him from saying that it should be postponed until the bishop was better. Once she'd bought the wood, they'd never be able to stop her.

She looked over the drawings once more. She'd order the wood today and start work as soon as the bird-cage was finished. Rose folded her drawings and walked out of the room.

"Rose!"

Elaine Heverson was coming down the hall towards her, her large eyes looking even larger than usual and focused on Rose as if the glance might hypnotize her or turn her to stone.

"Can we go somewhere?"

"What do you mean, Elaine?"

"Someplace private. That room you just came from. What is it?"

"Nothing yet. It's empty."

"We'll go in there."

She opened the door and pushed Rose through it.

"I just wanted to thank you."

"What for?"

"For not mentioning anything."

"What didn't I mention anything about?"

"I'm sure you knew. I could tell."

"Knew what?"

"About us. Gordon and I."

Rose looked at the woman, who appeared about to explode with nervous energy.

"You mean there's something between Gordon and you?"

"You knew. You must have known. After you met us the other day. You were in here, and you must have heard us out in the hall. We were right outside the door."

"I thought you were discussing a piece of music."

"Well we were, but there was more to it than that."

"Well, Elaine, I didn't notice."

"You must have. We all know that you're very astute, Rose. The bishop's eyes and ears."

"I'm not the bishop's spy. And I guess I'm less astute than you gave me credit for being."

Elaine stared at her. She looked as if she might cry.

"And now I've blurted it out."

"There's no reason for me to tell anyone."

"Oh, Rose, you're so good. After I've been such a dim-wit."

She was chewing her lower lip as if it were a piece of soft candy.

"Are you shocked?" she asked.

"I'm a little surprised," Rose said. "I didn't think Gordon was interested in women."

"Everybody thinks that about men who lead boys' choirs."

"It is a cliché, isn't it?"

"It's what I thought at first, I must admit. But I thought he was so wonderful, and I could save him from it."

She seemed to mean the words. She found him wonderful. Wonderful. Rose was astonished.

"What about the proposal he made to the bishop? For a version of *Don Giovanni,* with the boys playing the women's roles. That hardly sounds like an idea that a perfectly normal man would concoct."

"It was deliberate," Elaine said. "One night we were in the choir library together, and somebody nearly caught us, one of the choir mothers, and I told Gordon he had to do something. I was sure everybody must know, and I said he had to do something so no one would suspect. Well he knows that people think he's gay. It amuses him. So he concocted this idea for a homosexual *Don Giovanni*, and said that once the word got around, we'd never have to worry. Nobody would have any doubts about him after that."

"Then why did you think I'd be so sure to know after seeing you talking in the hall?"

"Just something about you, Rose. I felt as if you could see right through me. I've always felt that way about you. Every time you look at me, I'm sure you know everything I'm thinking."

"Well it's not true, Elaine. I have at least the average level of stupidity and insensitivity. The bishop's the one with X-ray vision."

"Really? I always thought of him as off on his own somewhere, talking to God."

"I'm sure he does that too, but he has a pretty sharp eye. Or had."

"How is he?"

"Much the same."

"I really do want Gordon to write that piece of music. It would mean so much to everyone in the diocese. Henry's so well loved."

"I had the feeling people think he's odd. Eccentric and flighty. Not down to earth."

"But that's how a bishop should be. One foot in heaven."

"So is Gordon going to write this piece?"

"I don't know. He doesn't really believe in his talent. He's far too modest."

"That's not my impression."

"It's true, Rose. I've come to know him."

"So you've said."

"I just couldn't help it."

She was blushing, and the wen at the side of her nose was more noticeable. Rose wondered why she'd never had it removed. She seemed the sort of woman who would.

"You won't tell?"

"I'm not much inclined to interfere in other people's lives."

"Bob's a good man," Elaine said, "and an excellent father, but . . . he's a bit predictable."

"I suppose we all are, after a while."

"But Bob thinks it's a virtue. He thinks that's the way people ought to be."

"It makes things more comfortable, I suppose."

"I don't want to be comfortable. Do you? I know it won't last, with Gordon. He won't stay at the cathedral forever, will he? He has a career to make. But while he's here, someone special like Gordon, it's an honour to be part of his life."

Rose stared at the woman, the quick little body, the pendulous breasts, and felt astonishment at the words she was hearing. She felt as if Elaine, the efficient, twittering choir guild mother, were drunk or doped. She was saying the most extraordinary things. She was quite lunatic with passion.

"I won't tell anyone what's going on between you and Gordon, and if I see you together, I'll turn my back."

"Thank you, Rose. Perhaps I can return the favour someday."

"That seems unlikely," Rose said.

As they came out the door into the hall, Gordon appeared, walking towards them.

"Gordon," Elaine said, "Rose is an absolutely wonderful person."

Gordon looked confused.

"Elaine sees virtues in people that they don't really have," Rose said. "But you must already know that."

She turned away from the two lovers before either of them could speak and went through the church to the basement to have one more look at the books and papers for which she was making a home. It was a sunny day, and the cathedral was exceptionally bright. One or two worshippers knelt in the pews, praying silently, telling God their secrets. Rose wished that Elaine had confided in God rather than blurting out to Rose the news of her affair. If she had never been told, then she wouldn't have to scold herself now for refusing to take it seriously, for mocking something that was important to those immersed in it.

Chappie was in his room, working on the same paperback. He looked up as Rose helped herself to the worklight on its extension.

"What's the average gestation period of an elephant?" he asked.

"I have no idea."

"Six hundred and twenty-four days."

"Why?"

"What do you mean, Why?"

"Why is it six hundred and twenty-four days?"

Chappie looked puzzled.

"Well I suppose that's how long it takes," he said.

Rose held out her hand.

"Give me the key to that padlock, and I'll let you get back to your book."

Chappie passed her a key, without speaking, and turned away. She had upset him.

Rose plugged in the extension and dragged the cord behind her as she made her way to the little storage room. Inside, she felt the dampness of stone and age wrap itself around her skin, the smell of must clog her nose. The moulds and fungi came out of the earth and found the books, those little dances of letters that were the voice of the spirit; the spores landed on the pages and sought the other life of the paper, its organic source, and tried to draw it back down into the ground.

Rose began to sort and measure. When she started to plan the archive, she'd thought there might be some wonderful secret hidden in these old books, a new gospel, a lost letter of Paul, but there was nothing startling. The ledgers contained figures, and the schoolbooks, notes for talks to Sunday school students. Rose made an accurate survey and then closed the room. As she snapped the lock, she thought she heard something from a back corner of the basement. A voice humming or singing. She lifted the work-light and carried it into the dark space in front of her. To one side she saw a small closet full of old choir gowns. She walked to the end of the cord and found a nail to hang the work-light. To one side of her lay a pile of old organ pipes, left here when the cathedral organ was last restored. She walked farther over the dirt floor, but the sound was gone now, and she couldn't see clearly as she went farther from the light. Yet she was sure that she had heard a human voice somewhere here. Perhaps she had finally gone mad.

Something moved to her left. It must be one of the wild cats. She stood still and listened. All she could hear was footsteps from above.

In this dream, Henry is the dreamer watching himself. Behind him there is some kind of crowd, visible because he is flying above, as Ishakak has told him a shaman can do, seeing the mighty procession of spirits guiding the man, a cloud of witnesses gathered to support his journey. Suddenly some kind of bad news spreads among them like a blast of wind, and like trees in a hurricane, they bend and one after another are torn loose. The darkness comes close to the one who has lost all contact with the loving spirits among the dead, and now the wind is a darkness, is pulling away pieces of his skin and hair, pieces of flesh.

Then, as he tries to hold the earth, and as the dreamer begins to feel the pull of wind on his body as well, he sees two figures blown past, their bodies joined and tumbling like weeds with a wild flailing of arms and legs. He tries to speak gently to them, but the words are torn from his mouth and make no sense.

He was at his mother's bedside, aware that she was dying, and then suddenly he was awake, aware of the light from the street falling on his wall. The dream of his mother's bedside had been very real, more a memory than a dream. She had died not long after he had come back from the army. He sat by her, as he had in the dream. He knew, when he visited her, that there was something she wanted to talk about; at first she couldn't bring herself to it; but finally she mentioned Amelia.

"We knew," she said, "that it wasn't right. She was full of some desperate, dark thing that she thought was love, but we could see that it wasn't. We tried our best to be good to her, you know."

Then she was silent, and at first Henry wasn't sure why she had spoken, but as he heard her words now in his mind, he knew. She wanted him to feel that not all the guilt was his, and what she had said helped. Sometimes it would come back to him on days when his body was infected with a sense of sinfulness that was like a disease. Her love was a presence that helped him escape, and over the years Henry had learned that the body-crawling horror wasn't sin but only a kind of unhappiness. Sin wasn't an aspect of melodrama, the stage devil with his fireworks and fake smoke. Sin was as ordinary as a picnic on the riverbank in bright sunlight, for its life was in the solitude of each human being. The stone at the bottom of the heart. Nothing more, in a way, than a kind of absent-mindedness, a loss of concentration, a wandering of attention.

Was there sin in what had happened to Amelia? Somehow, he had betrayed her, led her to places where she was too far from home, and when she was gone, he had betrayed her again by the ease with which he had found comfort. She had gone into the barest room of her soul and sat down there and sought for what would maintain her in the face of the echoing emptiness of the long arctic night. She had gone by herself into that bare room and she had never emerged.

A bare room. With no access to power, to glory, to light, to music. The blindness in which the eye stops at the surface and can see nothing beyond. The deafness when God is only a word.

Sleep comes on him again, and he is aware of watching himself dream, watching himself go out of his own control into the grip of something else. Downward, the pressure forcing him down and making him small. He is one of a group of seals swimming under the water, their soft bodies undulating through the dim nether sky. Sometimes one of the other seals swims close to him, and the two bodies touch as they move. He understands that they are going downward to visit the goddess, and as he swims he tries to remember her name, reciting Inuit words to himself, but the name will not come back.

He presses down deeper into the water, which is of a heavy blackness, and he is now alone. It is cold, harder to swim, his body stiff and moving only with difficulty. The goddess is near, and she is watching him with harsh eyes. Henry knows that he is being observed, though he himself can see nothing, and he turns his body in the gloom of ocean in the hope of confronting the goddess creature who is there. Slowly he realizes that she is below him, but when he looks down, all he can see is dirt and foulness, and then he knows that these are the filthy emanations from the misdeeds of men and women. He remembers how Ishakak told him that each time a taboo is broken, more filth clings to the body of the goddess. She lies like a huge soft suppurating wound on the floor of the sea beneath him. Her eyes are invisible under the dirt, yet Henry can feel that they are watching him. They are the eyes of one woman who sees all his laughable weaknesses and records them and suffers for them and waits. She will always know him; he will always be known, there is no escape from what she has seen of him.

Rose had worked late into the evening on the bird-cage, taken the tiny wooden bird home with her, sat in her apartment after midnight painting it the bright yellow and black of a goldfinch. As she flipped through an illustrated field guide to North American birds, the tiny lemony finch had taken her fancy. She remembered seeing small flocks of them in the weedy fields near their house when she was a girl, their quick dashing bursts of flight from plant to plant. The goldfinch was a bird of the rich summer fields, and perfect to hang in the bishop's room.

The cage was finished and she had come in early this morning to put on one more coat of wax. The sliding panels gave it the inner rhythm she'd hoped for, as if it had rooms for all occasions. It was possible to reach in through the panel openings and place the bird, on his wire legs, in any one of the sections. The bird's eyes were the shiny black ends of drawing pins, and these gave him gaiety and glitter, but she'd deliberately carved him a bit crudely. She wanted a magical wooden bird, not an ersatz budgie. No one but the bishop would understand the point of it, but she hoped that he would; or at worst he would know that it was a gift and that she had made it.

She rubbed the waxed hardwood once more with a soft cloth, set the goldfinch on his perch and lifted the cage. As she held it up, she turned it and looked at the wooden bird from all the cage's angles. There was a briskness about him; he was a speck of sunlight, contained but not imprisoned. Yes. She liked him.

Rose went upstairs to her desk. She heard Frank on the telephone in his office, and she saw the day-nurse's car parked out the front.

She'd take the bird-cage up right now, this minute.

When she reached the bishop's room, the nurse was just helping him back into bed after the laborious trip to the bathroom. Ishakak sat in the corner by the window, staring at a spot on the wall, his head nodding slowly, a slight humming sound coming through the room, as if he were chanting very softly under his breath. The skull and the other amulets still lay on the table, but most of the tobacco was gone, and there was a smoky smell to the room. After the bishop was settled in bed, she looked towards him and caught his eye, then held out the cage.

"I brought you a pet," she said. She went closer to

him and turned the cage around so he could study it, and see the bird.

"I wanted to make a bird-cage, but I didn't think you needed a real bird to worry about so I carved this little fellow."

The bishop's face changed, the half that wasn't paralyzed, moved. It hurt Rose that his lovely smile was so slow and trapped now, not the wide quick flash she had known in the past. Still, it was good that he was pleased. Rose put the case on the chest opposite the bed.

"Later on I'll find a way to hang it up."

The nurse was looking at it, poking her finger in towards the bird as if it were real.

"Isn't it sweet?" she said. "Did you get a pattern from a magazine?"

"No." Rose wanted to kick the woman.

Ishakak was studying the cage, and especially the bird.

"Is that a picture of your helper?" he said, in his curiously flat voice.

"No," Rose said. "I don't have a helping spirit. Just Jesus."

The bishop was watching her, and listening.

"Henry told us that Jesus was a pretty strong spirit. But he's the white man's spirit."

Rose heard footsteps on the stairs as Ishakak was speaking. Whoever it was moved quickly, almost ran up the stairs.

Curwan Brant appeared at the door. His neck seemed

longer than ever, and there was something almost deranged about his expression.

"Edgar Worral has just told me," he said, "what's been going on here."

The nurse looked at the tall figure in black with a clerical collar, looming in the doorway as if he might be about to call down a curse on the whole establishment. She looked to Rose for help.

"Calm down, Curwan. What's going on is that I just brought the bishop this bird-cage that I made for him."

"Don't pretend to innocence, Rose. I know what's been happening and I know that you're responsible. There will be a calling to account in due time."

"Are you going to have me burned at the stake? Or is stoning a better idea?"

Curwan ignored Rose's words as he strode across the room to where Ishakak was sitting.

"It's time for you to leave," he said.

Ishakak studied Curwan then said something in Inuktitut and started to laugh quietly.

"What did he say?" Curwan asked.

"You'd have to ask Henry," Rose said. "He's the only one who understands."

"What did you say?" Curwan said to Ishakak.

The old man looked at him with a wide smile that showed his broken and missing teeth. He spoke again in his own language. It was a long speech, and at the end, he was still smiling.

"What did he say?"

"I don't know," Rose said.

"He's mocking me."

"He might just be telling you a good joke."

"This is no time for jokes."

"I don't know why not."

"The bishop's soul is in danger."

"What in the world do you mean?"

"This is the devil's work, to sow confusion in the mind of a dying man, to draw his soul away from Christ. What this Eskimo is doing is witchcraft. It is the service of dark spirits."

Ishakak spoke again in Inuktitut, as if in answer to what Curwan was saying.

"Ishakak is an old friend of Henry's. He offers what he can, in his own way."

Curwan had seen the skull now.

"Look at that," he said. "Witchcraft. Devil worship."

"*Memento mori*," Rose said.

"Excuse me," the nurse said, "but this kind of excitement isn't very good for the patient. Perhaps you could have your discussion in the other room."

Ishakak's voice continued in the background, speaking softly and cheerfully, words that were incomprehensible to the rest of them. Curwan seized him by the arm and tried to drag him out of the chair.

"Stop that," Rose said.

'Couldn't we go in the other room?" the nurse repeated.

"He must be driven out," Curwan said. He stood over

Ishakak's chair, his eyes wild, his whole figure, Rose thought, almost prophetic, as if he had lived his life waiting for this moment. She glanced towards the bed. The bishop's good hand was clasped hard on the covers, and his face looked as if he might be struggling to speak. He couldn't defend himself; Rose must be his champion.

"Curwan," Rose said, "you can't just walk in here and begin to manhandle a friend of the bishop's."

"Henry is no longer responsible. We must do what's best for him."

"And you know what's best for him, do you?"

"What's best for him is to die in Christ."

"You have no idea when he's going to die, and you have no business trying to remove Ishakak when Henry wants him here."

"How do you know Henry wants him?"

"I asked him and he wrote yes."

"In his weakness, he's given in to temptation."

He had grabbed hold of Ishakak's shirt and began trying to pull him out of the chair.

"Really," the nurse was saying, "I don't think this is advisable. All this shouting. The patient is supposed to be kept quiet. I can't be responsible."

"When I expel this sorcerer," Curwan said, "you can have all the quiet you like."

He tried to lift Ishakak who was holding the arms of the chair and smiling as if this were a child's game.

"Is this your idea of Christian love, Curwan?"

" 'I come to bring not peace but a sword!' " Curwan

recited loudly and gave Ishakak a tug. His shirt was twisted out of shape, and the picture of Mick Jagger appeared to be winking.

"What gives you the right," Rose said, "to decide who your bishop can have for company?" She could feel the anger beginning to stiffen her body, and she was afraid she would start to beat Curwan with her fists. The only thing that held her back was the knowledge that she was strong enough to do him some permanent damage, though she would have rejoiced in that. She caught a glimpse of Henry's poor, pale clenched face, and she wanted to wound Curwan, to maim him for life.

"He can have company," Curwan said, "but not witch doctors."

He was panting now with the effort of trying to move the burly Inuit.

"Just what company?"

"Decent Christian men."

"And who's going to do the selection? You? He has no family. He has no children."

Curwan had let go of Ishakak's shirt for a moment. He stood, trying to get his breath.

"He's got one," Ishakak said, calmly, as if the whole scene had happened to someone else.

"One what?" Rose asked.

"A kid."

"What do you mean?"

"After Henry left, my wife had one that was pretty white. We figured he was Henry's."

"That's impossible," Rose said.

"She liked Henry. She never had a white man before."

"Are you telling me that your wife was Henry's. . .?" She couldn't find the word.

"We both liked Henry," Ishakak said cheerfully.

"And he has a son up there?"

"He works for the government. Pretty good job."

"Did Henry know about this?"

"I told him when I came."

"What about Henry's wife?"

"She was tired. She wanted to go to the Moon Spirit. When Henry didn't have a wife, I shared mine."

Rose began to feel dizzy and thought she was going to faint. She sat down on the side of the bed and closed her eyes. She felt a hand touch hers. It was Henry's good hand that he had stretched out to lie on hers. She looked towards him and saw that there were tears on his face.

"I knew Henry was concealing something evil," Curwan said. "I've suspected it for years. Got rid of his wife so he could take an Eskimo concubine. Little less than murder, I expect. Apart from the sins of the flesh. Mounted on some brown woman like a heathen. And that's the man they made a bishop. Well, he won't be a bishop for long."

"And why not?" Rose asked. She thought she might be screaming.

"I'll see to it," Curwan shouted. "I'll have him removed from office."

"He's been consecrated," Rose said. She was holding Henry's hand.

"If we can deconsecrate a church," Curwan declaimed, "we can deconsecrate a bishop."

The dizziness in Rose's head suddenly concentrated itself into a blaze of anger. She rose from the bed and grabbed Curwan from behind, lifted him off the floor and began to drag him out of the room towards the stairs. She was going to hurl him down the stairs and kill him. Her grip on his thin chest was so tight that she knew she was pressing the old man's breath out of him. She enjoyed it. She wanted to see him fall and break and die. As she carried him across the room, his feet kicked at her shins and he reached back to pound at her with his fists, to pull her hair. He was hurting her, but the pain only increased her rage. She heard the nurse's voice, somewhere in the distance.

"I don't think this is a good idea," the woman said.

Curwan kicked her. One of his blows struck the side of her face. She was close to the stairs now, and she knew that she might tumble down herself, but she hardly cared. She got him to the top step and threw his body sideways with a great heave of her powerful arms. She felt him start to fall and then there was a loud grunt. She looked down.

Frank Neal was halfway up the stairs, holding and steadying Curwan where he had caught him and saved him from disaster. Frank looked frightened and confused. Curwan was staring at her, his teeth bared.

"You are accursed, Rose," he was shouting. "You are a barren fig. Your flesh will be torn by dogs."

Three

The water ran brightly over her fingers as she lifted her hand from the bowl. Rose rubbed the blue cloth slowly over the bishop's chest. It cast a pale blue reflection on the skin. Little rivulets of water passed the dark nipples, poured through the scattering of white hairs. He lay with a towel at his side to catch any of the excess water. The skin was pale, slightly mottled, with here and there a chocolate-coloured mole.

Rose was the bishop's day nurse until the new one began tomorrow. The previous nurse had quit abruptly after the bedside battle. Rose was a little surprised to find that she herself hadn't been cast into outer darkness as a result of her attempt to murder Curwan, but in an emergency Frank had shown that most remarkable characteristic of sensible people, he had been sensible. He got Curwan out of the house, and when Ishakak suggested that maybe it was time he got back to the Arctic, Frank had agreed and given him bus fare to Ottawa where he could catch a flight north. He had tried to calm the nurse, but she was hysterically determined to leave and wouldn't relent. Frank told Rose that the woman had agreed not to gossip about matters in the bishop's apartment, and Rose suspected that he had paid a large bribe to procure her silence. A very temporary silence, Rose was sure.

When the bishop woke from sleep to discover that Ishakak had gone, with all his feathers and bones, his skull, he seemed at first stricken, and Rose was stabbed with guilt, but now he had accommodated himself to the shaman's absence.

She dipped the cloth again, soaped it and washed the bishop's paralyzed arm, startled at how perfect it was, the blood pulsing beneath the skin, the muscles only a little loose with age. Yet it was shut off from the brain, lapsed and silent, alive yet not alive. She lifted the useless hand and washed it, rinsed the cloth in the bowl of water.

The drops of water that fell back into the bowl as she squeezed the cloth caught flashes of sun from the window and reflected them, each drop a tiny mirror. She rinsed the hand and arm. Useless. Useless. A hard word, and yet true; no wish would make it less so.

It was a pleasure to wash the bishop's body. Too seldom Rose touched human flesh, but she wasn't one for the indiscriminate hugging of acquaintances, and she had no intimates. She held his useless arm in her own strong, four-fingered hand as she dried him with the towel. The skin was warm against hers. He could not feel her touch.

She put the arm down on the bed and walked to the other side. Here, he could move and feel. This was the hand the bishop had placed on hers. Had he touched her to give comfort or take it? Perhaps there was never any distinction. It was a process of induction, not flow.

At first he had watched her as she washed him, but now he lay with his eyes closed. He seemed weaker in the days since the battle that had taken place around his bed; his face was wan, his eyes dim.

She put a towel under his body and washed this side of his chest, her hand caressing the curving bones of the ribs; the flesh moved beneath the cloth. She could feel the beating of his heart against her fingers, and she was terribly, painfully aware that another life was lived inside the body she cared for, a life that was not hers. His. He was this man. Henry. *Henry, our bishop.* He was the beating of this other heart.

She lifted his arm and soaped the white hair in his armpit, rinsed it. Washed the arm and dried it and then set the bowl of water beside the bed as she prepared to turn him over to wash his back.

As she put her arm under the bishop's shoulders, his eyes opened and met hers, and he moved the good arm and leg to help her. When he was on his stomach, the paralyzed arm was caught beneath his body, and she reached under and pulled it loose. The man had broad shoulders, and even with the thickening of flesh that age had brought to the lower back, the torso angled in at the waist. On his shoulders were a few freckles, pale brown with a hint of green, the colour of a newborn fawn in the reflected light of the deep forest; the skin between them was a pearl white, with a slight translucency. Rose brought back the water and washed his back, wondering as she did, whether, since the stroke, he was aware of a clear borderline where feeling ended, or whether there was a no man's land of sensations half perceived, a pattern of perception that might be mapped on his skin in white, black, various shades of grey. She dried the bishop's back and rubbed lotion on it to help prevent bedsores.

To turn him from his front and lift him into a sitting position proved a difficult task. Rose was sure that nurses must have some set of tricks, and she was aware that she was manhandling him as if he were a particularly ungainly piece of furniture that she had to set in place to repair, but with the assistance of his good arm, she got him into a seated position without breaking anything. She put his pyjama jacket on, and as she was about to button it, she felt Henry's good hand push hers away, and he buttoned it himself, looking at her afterwards.

"Very impressive," Rose said. "I'll soon be able to set you to work at my turning lathe."

She helped him to lie back down, and pulled back the sheet that covered his lower body.

"Now we'll do the other half," Rose said and slid down the bottoms of the pyjamas. The bishop had closed his eyes again, and she wondered if it embarrassed him to have the privacy of his body exposed to her. Well, it was to be done, and Rose could see no point in making a fuss over it, but then she'd never been one to make a fuss over men's appendages. She had limited experience and not a great deal of interest. As she washed the bishop's feet and glanced up the long slender legs to the little huddle of wrinkled things in their nest of crinkly white hair, she

thought of Ishakak's light-skinned son, fathered by these comical organs when they were young and full of sap.

"The dean is planning his special prayer service for next week," Rose said to the bishop as she worked. "Tuesday seems the likeliest day."

Because he couldn't speak, Rose found herself too often subsiding into silence when she was with the bishop. She had to remind herself that he could hear and think.

"Some of the outlying parts of the diocese are sending carloads."

Washing the man's flesh, aware of how close the enormity of death might be, now that it had sunk its talons into a part of him, Rose was tangled in mysteries. At Morning Prayer, she repeated that she believed in the resurrection of the dead; at Communion that she looked for the resurrection of the dead and the life of the world to come, unsure just what the words meant. As she touched his body, helpless, mortal, she seemed to see it grow younger, long and slender and shining, the arms stretching upward to praise the God of light.

As his mother stroked his body with the wet cloth, Henry believed that he was dying. He lay naked on his bed, and his mother, over and over, wet his skin, and he understood that she was anointing him for death, cleansing him so that he would meet God in a state of perfection. His mother's face came close to him, and her eyes were huge, gentle and fearful, and then she was far away, dim and fading and miles above him. She was going away. Vanishing.

Her eyes were close again. It was late, but she would not sleep so that she might be with him when he died and went to heaven.

Around the throne of God in heaven
Shall countless children stand,
Children whose sins are all forgiven,
A holy, happy band.

He could hear her voice talking to his father about fever. He wanted her to touch him again, for his body was thick and swollen, and when he tried to breathe, there was a weight on his chest.

She was looking down at him. She was anointing his body. She would stay with him until he died, but he didn't want to die. He wanted to stay with his mother and father and Alice-Alice.

He liked the water on his skin. His skin was on fire, and the water cooled it. Henry was afraid that this was the fire of Hell and that his mother couldn't put the fire out. He knew it was wrong that he hadn't told them that he was sick just because he wanted to go to the circus, and as soon as he got among the crowd, he knew something bad was going to happen. It was hard to watch the circus people and everything he saw frightened him.

At first it was thrilling too. It made him shake inside, and when he looked at the elephants, they were so big and so strange that it seemed they might walk right into his eyes. The clowns were staring at him as if to ask him why he wasn't laughing, but he couldn't laugh; there was a thing too tight inside him, and if he laughed it would break. When the acts performed in more than one ring at once, he couldn't tell which to look at, and his eyes wouldn't focus, and the trick dogs were blurred.

The men on the trapeze swung through the air, and he gasped with fear every time they let go, and each time he saw them falling and wanted to rush out to catch the falling body, but he couldn't move, and he knew the big bodies of the men would crush him, and when he thought of that, his head spun with giddiness. He knew he was very sick,now, and he was afraid he might vomit. He closed his eyes, but when he did that he was falling from a trapeze and he opened them quickly to stop.

Right in front of them was a man who was bending his body into strange shapes. He put his legs behind his neck and walked on his hands. As Henry watched the contortions, he could feel each of his own limbs get heavier. His hands and feet were going farther away from him. The man bent down and wrapped one of his arms around his leg. Henry was afraid the contortionist was going to get stuck in one of his positions and would have to spend his life locked in a grotesque posture. A clown walked by, his face was huge and mocking, and then Henry felt something awful start in his head, and he fell from his seat.

Now he was lying on his bed, and his mother was bathing him with cool water to put out the fires. Henry remembered the contortionist. The man was turning into a huge snake.

Henry could hear his heart beating all through his body.

Everything inside him was swollen and trying to break out of his skin. There was a picture on the wall at school of a man with his stomach and chest open so you could see inside, and all over his body there were roads and pathways where the blood went, red and blue lines. The head lay on one side, the eyes closed, and the whole head was covered with red and blue lines. His heart was purple and had big red and blue pipes leading in and out. He was like a map with hundreds of rivers. Henry could feel the rivers running all through his body. He could hear the blood as it rushed out of the heart. All over his body were little rivers and streams like the ones in the swamp north of town, tiny streams invisible in the high grass until you stepped in them. Tiny fish and tadpoles rushed across the mud bottoms to hide in the grass and weeds, leaving a swirl of brown mud behind them.

When you died, you turned into mud, and then God came and got you and put your body together again and sent you to Heaven. And God took your soul to Heaven when you died. Henry was frightened of God taking the soul out of his body. The man in the school picture was wide open and you could see the parts inside, curved shapes and ugly colours. Henry could never be sure if the man was alive or dead. He must be dead because there were pictures of his heart cut open with something like string castles inside. On one side of his body, you could see the bones inside his arms and legs, the skull beneath the face. Henry tried to move his own arms and legs to feel the bones, but he couldn't. He couldn't move.

The contortionist turned into a snake, and now the snake was swimming along the red and blue rivers and eating the fish and tadpoles. If the snake was swimming inside him, it must be his soul. Henry didn't understand how God could take the snake into Heaven.

He could feel his mother washing him. She was washing him in the Blood of the Lamb to prepare him for death. Henry tried to see the Blood on his skin, but he couldn't lift his head.

Once in the butcher shop, he saw the butcher take out the inside parts of a chicken. The butcher cut it open with a knife and reached in his hand to pull out the organs. They were wet and shiny. The chicken was eviscerated.

The man on the wall at school was eviscerated, but God hadn't taken out all the organs. Henry didn't want to be eviscerated. He wanted his mother to stay with him and to cool the fire that was burning him.

Henry was frightened. He was frightened of everything. He was afraid he was even frightened of God.

But he would fall asleep, and when he woke, the sun would be shining, and his mother sitting by his bed, smiling at him, and he would smile back.

Henry opened his eyes, and watched as Rose pulled the white sheet up over him again. She smiled down at him and brushed his hair back into place with her rough, skillful hands. Then she took the bird-cage that she had brought him and hung it from a wire attached to a hook in the ceiling. The little wooden bird stared at him, like a bird he had seen, a bird in a painting, a bird in a garden.

A cardinal, a pair of cardinals, Amelia's cardinals, the back of the male a rich brown, the scarlet vestment of his front a revelation. A bright flash too on the short forceful beak of the female. The colours of a painting. The painting is Florentine. The face of the Madonna. The eyes hooded, face curving in towards a small chin, curving eyebrows and eyes and cheek. The gown such a dark blue that the eye saw it as no colour. Brown and gold. Soft shining gold.

The light was gold over the parsonage garden. Her face golden as it turned to him. Her eyes moved to him as he came in the gate.

The Christ is a young boy, standing upright, naked, and he exists on a different plane from the mother. An awkwardness of draughtsmanship. Or a statement about the child's separateness, even at such an early age.

At first one almost overlooked the bird. As he had, coming into the garden, seeing her there. The Child is holding a bird in his left hand, and the bird's bright eye is staring out of the picture. Brown and red, the colour of the cardinals, but smaller. A finch, icon of the crucifixion.

The parsonage garden where Amelia stood was a green so intense it was almost golden. He looked at her face, and how she smiled and behind her he noticed the two cardinals, male and female. One on the fence, the other in a small tree.

They watched her, and she spoke to them, and they watched her fearlessly. They whistled brightly, speaking to her and she answered. She had tamed them with her gentleness, her love.

Rose was looking out the window by her desk when she saw Stan Butts wobbling up the street on his bicycle. An immense bouquet of flowers in his hand made it difficult for him to steer, and Rose was afraid he'd tumble off and be run over before he arrived, but the bike lurched safely to the curb and Stan disentangled himself and his bouquet and pulled the bike up the curb with his free hand. He started towards the door, and Rose went out to meet him.

"Mildred and I thought perhaps it was time for some fresh blooms," Stan said as he saw her in the hall. "She cut these just this morning. The garden's done wonderfully well this year."

"There's a vase in the bedroom," Rose said. "Just toss out the old ones."

"I won't trouble him," Stan said. He held the flowers out to her. "You take them up sometime."

"He'd like to see you, Stanley. I'm sure he would."

"Peace and quiet," Stan said. "I'm sure he needs peace and quiet. After all that's happened."

"You've been talking to Curwan."

"He spoke to me."

"It was quite a scene."

"Curwan has always been rather . . . assertive. Very much the church militant."

"I suppose he could charge me with assault if he wanted."

"No, no. Nothing like that. The church keeps its own counsel about these things."

"Curwan had no business interfering."

"I'm sure that's true, Rose, but he thought it was for the best. Something of the warrior-priest about old Curwan, isn't there?"

He was smiling slyly at her. Rose had the impression that he was secretly delighted that she had tried to throw Curwan downstairs.

"How is the bishop?" Stan said.

"Go up and see."

"No, I shouldn't. I really shouldn't."

"He'd like to see you. If he's asleep, just change the flowers."

"Do you think so?"

"Of course."

"You're sure?"

"I'm judging by myself, Stan. It always makes me feel good to see you. I assume Henry feels the same way."

"What a lovely thing to say, Rose."

His eyes were filling with water. With a practised gesture, he pulled out a handkerchief and dried them.

"Mildred and I have been praying for him," he said. "One wonders just what to pray for, recovery, or peace of mind, or a good death, but I find that 'Thy Kingdom come, Thy will be done' pretty well sums it up."

"Take him the flowers."

Stan nodded and turned to the stairs. Rose went back to her desk and sat down to a pile of letters. It was hard to take them seriously. Her mind returned to the bishop in his bed upstairs, the pallor and weakness of his face. She was tempted to call a doctor, but she knew that would likely mean a return to hospital. Would he live the longer for it, or be any happier?

She was glad he would have fresh flowers in the room. Odd that one gave flowers to both the convalescent and the dead. Was there something ominous in the resemblance of a sick-room to a funeral? A body lost in flowers.

Lost in flowers. She'd forgotten. Joanne's story. She'd let it slip out of her mind.

They'd come out of church one day, she and Joanne, discussing the extra flowers by the pulpit which had been left from a parishioner's funeral the day before. As soon as they were on the street Joanne announced she had something to tell her and led the way up to the main street of town where they each bought an ice cream cone and carried it to the park at the corner.

"You mustn't ever tell anyone this," Joanne said.

"Tell anyone what?"

"Promise you won't tell. Mother still thinks we'll get sent to reform school if anyone finds out. She'll kill me if she hears I've told you."

"What's this all about?"

Joanne's quick little tongue licked the chocolate ice

cream that was beginning to run down the cone.

"Do you promise?" she said.

"Yes. Of course. Now tell me."

Joanne licked her ice cream cone again, and her eyes turned mischieviously to Rose and then away as she launched into her tale. It was a lovely story she told, of how they had once lived in a house across from a large cemetery. Joanne wasn't allowed to cross the street, but her brother, who was two years older, was. He and his friends often went into the cemetery to play, and one day, as Joanne had stood on her side of the roadway looking longingly across at the beautiful flowers decking a recent grave, her brother, in an uncharacteristic moment of generosity, offered to bring her some. Once he and his friend began to deliver them, they got carried away. Inside the garage was a child's table and chairs where Joanne played in rainy weather. By the time their mother got home from shopping, Joanne was enthroned on one of the chairs, which her brother had set on top of the little table, and Joanne, the table and the chair were covered with floral tributes. Joanne was convinced, she said, that she had become a princess, and as the two boys brought more and more flowers to adorn her, she understood the delight of royalty. They had her all but buried in roses and gladioli and chrysanthemums when their mother arrived home. When she learned the source of the flowers, she plucked Joanne off the table, collected the flowers in a plastic garbage bag, swatted both children and swore them to secrecy.

A week later, the neighbourhood newspaper carried a report deploring vandalism at the local cemetery. Their mother read it aloud to them and painted a dark picture of what would happen to them all if anyone ever learned the truth.

"I've never told a soul," Joanne said. "Not till today."

"You must have looked wonderful."

"I felt like such a princess," Joanne said. "Such a perfect and wonderful princess."

"You are," Rose said. "You are a princess. You even lick your ice cream like a princess, with dainty little licks."

"Oh, poop," Joanne said. "You're just feeling jealous again, and whenever you get jealous, you tell me how sweet I am."

"Jealous?" Rose said. "Why should I be jealous of you?"

"Because everybody thinks I'm an angel. I could see you getting jealous after church when the rector was talking to me."

"Your mother doesn't think you're an angel."

"No, but your mother does."

"One of these days she'll catch on to you."

"I hope not. It's nice to be treated like an angel."

"I'll never know."

"Not until you die and go to heaven."

"I'm not getting my hopes up about that either. God probably prefers little blue-eyed blondes."

Joanne was suddenly serious.

"You shouldn't talk like that, Rose. Not about God."

"But I do. I do talk like that about God. That's why I'll never get to be an angel."

Joanne didn't answer. She got up from the bench, and they walked through the park and went to Rose's house for lunch.

Rose sat at her desk, in her mind a picture of Joanne among the flowers, blue eyes staring out of the lavish heap of brilliantly coloured petals, the gift, the given, earth's ornament, the child of spring and love. Stan Butts put his head in the doorway.

"He was asleep, Rose," he said. "I didn't wake him. He doesn't look well, does he?"

"No."

"Has the doctor been?"

"The new nurse is coming tomorrow. I'll ask her if she thinks we should call."

Stan waved and left. Rose watched him out the window. The fenders on his bicycle were loose and rusty, and he climbed on and began to peddle with great gentleness, as if he felt immense sympathy for the bicycle's state of age and decrepitude and hardly dared expect it to carry him. He wobbled into traffic and was gone. Rose tried to work. What she really wanted was to start on the shelves and cupboards for the archive. If she finished them, even the basic construction, she could borrow a polaroid camera and take a picture to show the bishop. She'd spend the whole evening in her workshop, she decided, and get a good start.

Norman knew for sure they were after him now. They

shone lights at him, and all last night the machines screamed from the other end of the Pipe Hole. Norman was lying in his corner, and he covered his head with his shirt to try to shut them out. He couldn't stop them. When he closed his eyes, he could feel Thy Spirit and the Dark Angels were coming close and whispering. The Dark Angels were invisible; they were all around but he couldn't see them, and he hit out to drive them away, but he only hurt his hand on the stone.

Norman put his shirt over his head again and tried to imagine what it would be like when Glory came back to be to him, but he was afraid she never would. Maybe somebody told her what he did to the white cat, and she didn't understand that he was mad because she went away and because the cat hurt him with its claws. Maybe Glory wouldn't be to him at all. He could feel Thy Spirit and the Holey Ghost waiting for him at the end of his tunnel, and he pulled the messenger pigeon and Glory's picture of Elvis close to him to try to remember when they were together and Glory went down on her knees to beg him to be good.

Norman couldn't remember. He knew the memory was there somewhere, but he couldn't get hold of it. Something was happening in his stomach and his chest. The Holey Ghost was inside him and making a hole that would get bigger and bigger until he was nothing and all his insides would come out with white worms like the pigeon.

Norman could feel how the white cat was soft in his

hands after he killed it. It was so soft that he wanted to stroke it, but he hated it too and threw it down and ran away.

The hole inside him was getting bigger.

He wanted to run away, but he was waiting, he was waiting for one of the messenger pigeons to come, but when he tried to listen for the messenger pigeon to come, all he would hear was the Dark Angels whispering, and he was afraid of what the Holey Ghost was doing inside of him.

Norman lifted his head out from under his shirt to listen for the messenger pigeons. He wondered if the sound he heard in his head was the messenger pigeons. He couldn't tell what it was saying. He sat perfectly still and didn't breathe to try to hear the sound better, but the quieter he got the quieter the whispering got. They were teasing him.

He held his breath as long as he could, and while he was holding it, he knew that he had to get away from his corner in the Pipe Hole. They had the lights and the machines; they knew where to find him, so they could come any time they wanted. Norman listened hard. He couldn't tell if the soft voice was inside his head or was coming from somewhere else.

He had never thought before that when the pigeons brought their message, it might be in pigeon language so you'd never know what they were saying. Maybe that's why there used to be millions of pigeons and they went away, because nobody could understand what they said. When they went away, they turned into Dark Angels to go inside your head.

When the pigeon talk started inside your head, there wasn't room for anything else.

Pigeon talk. Pigeon talk.

Norman tried to remember about Glory coming to be to him, but he couldn't. It wouldn't stay in his head. All he could hear was the message from the Dark Angels who talked in pigeon talk, and he couldn't understand. It would get soft and loud. He tried holding his breath again, but that just made another kind of noise in his head. The Holey Ghost was inside his head now.

He touched Elvis and the messenger pigeon, but it didn't help. The messenger pigeon was dead, and Glory said Elvis was dead, but Norman didn't believe it. When he saw his picture up on the wall, all shining, he didn't believe he was dead. Glory had a stereo and she had records of all his songs, and they listened to them together.

Norman felt better when he remembered that. The Dark Angels left him alone for him to remember Glory's records. But then they started again, whispering in pigeon talk that he couldn't understand.

The only thing was to get out of his corner. They showed him the lights and made him hear the machines so he'd know how close they were. The Lord was with Thy Spirit all the time now, and the only thing to do was to escape.

His corner wasn't safe any more. He started to crawl along the Pipe Hole towards the basement of the church, afraid that when he crawled from the Pipe Hole, the lights would be waiting and Glory would be to his father.

He wanted to take Elvis and the messenger pigeon with him. He knew he wouldn't be coming back to his corner, and when he thought of that, he started to cry. He tried to drag his things along the Pipe Hole, but because he was scared that when they put the lights on him he would have to run, and he couldn't run if he were carrying anything, he left them behind.

His hand was sore where he banged it on the stone when he tried to hit the Dark Angels.

He put his knee down on a sharp piece of stone. He was close to the opening now, and he waited to see if the lights would shine on him. It would be like the Hell Drivers when he ran out into the lights to do the clown act. You never knew who was watching because the lights were so bright in your eyes. You couldn't tell if they were laughing when you fell down and broke your tits.

Pigeon talk. Pigeon talk. Pigeon talk.

The Dark Angels were louder now. He was at the end of the Pipe Hole. He looked out. The only light was from one of the windows in front, near Chappie's room. The basement was empty, but Norman knew that Thy Spirit could hide anywhere. Even if they didn't come with the lights and machines, they were waiting for him. He wanted to go back to his corner and hide, but he knew he couldn't. The Holey Ghost had found him and would eat holes inside him until there was nothing left.

He went across the basement to the curving stairs. In

the corner he saw the cat watching him. Maybe he should touch it for luck. But when he moved towards it, the cat ran and disappeared into a hole in the wall. The cat was like Norman. He knew places to hide. Norman wondered if the Holey Ghost got inside the cat too.

Norman pulled open the wooden door that led to the curving stairs and walked slowly up. There was a kind of quietness that was like a shout. When he got to the top, he wanted to close his eyes, but he kept going across to the other door, the one where the stairs went inside the wall. He knew that behind him now, Thy Spirit was in the Pipe Hole and in Norman's corner, so he couldn't ever go back. He reached the top of the first stairs, turned in a little gallery where there were chairs piled, and flags, then started up the next set of stairs. It was hard to get his breath, but he kept climbing. They were close behind him, Thy Spirit and the Holey Ghost and the Dark Angels. They were coming behind him and if he stopped, they would catch him.

There was another, smaller gallery, and then more stairs, a long, narrow set of stairs. Norman could see daylight at the top where the windows were. They were little windows, down low. They had bumpy glass, and you couldn't see out.

When Norman got to the top of the stairs, he had to stand still to get his breath.

Up here, everything was bright. The sun was shining on the windows and making them glitter. Above him, was the dome of the church. It was blue, and it looked like the sky.

Norman started to get his breath and walked in a circle once round the dome. He always walked all around it once before he looked down. When he was halfway around, he started to hear the whispering in his head again, and then when he was almost back at the stairs, something flashed across in front of his eyes and made him shout.

It was a bird. It flew to the other side of the dome and landed.

Norman got back to where he'd started, and then he looked down. The church was empty. The sun was pouring in through the windows, and everything was shining where Bill and Chappie had polished it. The colours in the windows were bright. Norman stared at Jesus in his long dress and wondered if Jesus was frightened of Thy Spirit and the Holey Ghost. Jesus had his hands up as if he was going to do a dance. Norman put his hands up like that and did a little dance. It startled the bird and made it fly around. It went around and around the dome making little noises. Norman wondered if the bird would understand the whispering of the Dark Angels, and as soon as he thought about that, he could hear the pigeon talk in his head again, and he knew that it never stopped; even if he forgot to listen for a minute, it was always there. And he knew that the Holey Ghost was still inside him. He could feel the holes again now. And he knew that the Lord was with Thy Spirit and that Thy Spirit was coming up the stairs to find him. He could never go back down the stairs to the Pipe Hole. He could never go to sleep in his corner. Thy Spirit was everywhere now, and Norman couldn't go back.

When Norman looked down, he could see, a long way off, the candles, and where they put on their gowns to sing, and where they talked, and where they came up to kneel down, and all the shining brass and the polished wood and the light coming in all the windows. He could see red and blue and purple and the other colours around Jesus where he was dancing in his long dress. The bird was flying around in front of his eyes as he looked down, moving so fast Norman could hardly follow his movements.

If Norman put up his arms to dance like Jesus, they felt like the wings of the bird.

The bird didn't need to be frightened of Thy Spirit. He could fly so fast he could always get away. Norman watched how quickly he moved his wings.

Jesus was dancing in his window, and Norman was dancing too, and the bird was flying high up in the church. The bird wasn't frightened of Thy Spirit, and Jesus wasn't, and Norman wasn't, even though he could never go back down. But now that he was dancing with Jesus and the bird, it was like being back with the Hell Drivers, and the way it made him want to laugh. The bird was coming closer and closer to Norman and trying to show him something. It wasn't like the messenger pigeons. It wasn't just a noise in his head. He was following the bird and he was laughing. He didn't know who could see him, but he danced for them.

He didn't have a long dress like Jesus, but he felt as tall as Elvis and started to sing his songs. He was following the bird.

Norman was flying.

Something lavish, something extravagant about these gardens; they gobbled earth and sun and leapt into leaf and blossom. The soil was sodden with rain, the air soaked with light, and where they met, the grass was a glowing green, and the flower gardens were forests, feasts of God's love, clusters of climbing roses hanging from the trellises, little explosions of sky in the bachelor's buttons, geraniums like sprays of arterial blood.

He saw. He thought he saw. He saw. Lost in the light.

The earth in its old age conceived. Gold heart of the rose, gold of pollen, heavy bags on the legs of the bees.

A week after his ordination as bishop, he had come back home to celebrate communion in his first church. He had broken the bread and blessed the wine, and the server who had brought the lavabo to wash his fingers had his own young face.

He saw. He thought he saw. The lost figures of his father and mother somewhere back in the church, full of joy that their son had come among them as a bishop.

We are not worthy so much as to gather up the crumbs under thy table. A bee buried itself in the orange horn of the pumpkin flower, loaded itself in saffron dust and tumbled out into the air.

He turned a corner into a street, familiar, shaded by

the tall green parasols of the elms – leading to the bright glint of water.

She was not here.

He walked towards the water, where last night he had seen the fires on the shore. Men and women waited at the gates of their yards to greet him and call to mind the old days. The mauve blossoms of the clematis, the blue of morning glory, hung in stillness over the porches and walls. The wife of the people's warden brought him a sandwich, sliced pork, and a cup of tea. He ate and drank with her and passed on his way.

An old woman on a porch called him to her and sat him down on the wicker chair opposite her. She had a crocheted quilt over her knees, though it was a bright summer day. Cold death was seeking her out from her feet upward, she said. She liked to hear him play the cornet in the park on Sundays, she said. If he continued, he could be as fine a cornettist as Herbert L. Clarke.

On the lake, the boats of the fishermen moved quietly through the water that reflected the blue sky.

Dandelions like miniature suns.

He passed this way walking to school. Fred's house a block away. Cam Sleeth was hoeing his vegetable garden, bald, corpulent.

"Twilight Dreams," by Herbert L. Clarke. He put the cornet to his lips, formed the embouchure.

The earth was floating. At the edge of the road was a deep puddle from the rain the night before, and he stared down and saw his face, blurred in the dark mirror, and a pale streak of cloud in the sky above him. Her eyes watched him. He looked up; the earth was awash with the glory of light. Christ whose glory fills the skies.

He saw the child when he reached the park. She was perhaps twelve. She was watching him as he sat down on a bench, her face familiar. The dark eyes flecked with gold glanced towards him and then away. She stood perfectly still at the edge of dappled sunlight.

She pushed back her hair. The high domed forehead. Knowing it, so well, wounds him.

The park is swaying in the wind, like a dirigible tugging at the ropes that bind it to the earth, and he can hear a sound of music, the voices of women, a cornet doubling the melodic lines. He gestures to the little girl, asking her to come to him, and she does, avoiding his eyes. He searches for words.

"Do you go to church?"

"Yes, I go to St. Luke's."

"Have you been confirmed?"

"No. I'm not old enough yet."

"I'm a bishop. I'd come for your confirmation if you'd like that."

She doesn't answer. He thinks how he would have felt at eleven or twelve if a stranger had spoken these words to him.

"Don't be frightened of what I say. I don't mean to confuse you. But you look so much like your mother. I feel I know you."

"Yes," she says.

The grass at his feet thick and long and damp with life and growth.

"Is your mother with you?"

"Yes."

He sees her standing a few feet away, watching him as he talks with the child, and as he looks up, she comes close. There are a few strands of grey in her hair, wrinkles by the eyes and mouth. The face is different in some other way, it has a stillness, gives off a different kind of light, and he realizes that what he is seeing is happiness.

As their eyes meet, his heart beats fast. He knows that he cannot touch her; instead he reaches out to the child and strokes the silky hair.

Defend, O Lord, this thy child with thy heavenly grace.

The girl turns to him, and she seems less frightened now. Amelia sits beside him on the bench and they talk of the daily business of their lives over the last years. The child listens, and he can see that she is soon bored with this history of the world.

The Holy Spirit is gently shaking the leaves of the trees and one leaf falls into sunlight. A squirrel runs over the grass. Voices call him, call him.

When the mother and child are gone, he will begin to walk slowly towards the water, following the voice that he cannot quite hear, the pure sound detached from words and music. The sunlight one colour under the green shade of the trees, and another colour in the wide space over the water. The ground swaying in the wind.

He will walk through the glitter of sun, with the sure knowledge that he is observed and loved and that the voice that shimmers like light over the surface of his brain is a voice of peace. He has walked here before, and he knows that he is awaited, that a figure attends him at the shore of the lake. His face has felt the brightness and resonance of the cornet's sound echo from the silver instrument into the silver of his bones as his breath becomes music.

As he runs down the hill to the water, the music and the silence of the great lake will clap their hands together, and between them, he will fall into an explosion of sunlight and see the pale slender legs that stand where the beach of pebbles rolls down into the depths of the lake. Henry will stop and look at the figure who gazes to the lake's horizon, garments held above the water, lightly, in the hands.

Each breath a world created and destroyed. Time ending, beginning and ending again.

He will wait here on the beach of polished stones. He will wait as long as he must until the figure turns and he sees the beloved face and bends to wash the feet, water falling in bright drops over his fingers.

Four

The rising sun appears and touches the dome of the cathedral. The streets are still almost empty, but at that moment, a young woman on a pale blue bicycle rides by and looks up to see the silvery light as it begins to travel down from the tip of the dome to the wide green lawn. Two joggers run past, and then the area around the stately building is deserted again. The bright summer daylight spreads through streets which are as empty as if all human life had been mysteriously wiped out, leaving only the architectural remains of humanity, which, without continuous care, will slowly crumble away to ruins, to be found, ages later, by explorers from some other world.

Rose knew that she was being stupid and stubborn, but she always was, wasn't she, and her grief and anger made it worse. If only they had allowed her to build the coffin. Rose had startled herself by making a scene over it, shouting at Frank, but in spite of all that, it was not to be done. They would have a store-bought coffin. Well let them. She had made her gift, the shelves and cupboards of the cathedral archive, and she had sworn that they would be completed and in their place before the funeral began.

And they would. She had slept little the last four

nights, pausing in the darkness only to weep and curse, to let her eyes close in a chair for a few minutes. As her exhaustion increased, she began to expect that she would have some kind of accident, cut off another finger, a hand, but after four days, she was still whole, and the sections of the archive, the wood dark and shining, stood about her on the floor, waiting to be assembled and fastened in place. She had strapped the wall with one-by-three pine screwed into lead plugs sunk in the brick and plaster. The cupboards, when they were set in place, would be fastened to the strapping by concealed screws. Her gift, she hoped, would last as long as the building.

She had one lower section in place, ready to be locked to the wall, but she had to set a large shelf unit on top of it, and it was heavy, too heavy really. It was going to be a struggle to lift it into place without scratching the wood or breaking the glass doors.

Rose moved the unit into position on the floor. There was no doubt that she ought to have help, but her anger and defiance would give her strength. She would do it alone, not share any part of it, not take the chance that they might notice what she has done to the room and try to stop her. Frank and the dean were aware, in some vague way, of what she was up to, but neither suspected that the work was finished, the room remade without their opinion being asked. She had put the last coat of wax on the finished wood the evening before, then gone home to eat and let herself sleep for an hour, coming back after midnight, when the cathedral and the diocesan centre were deserted, to transport the units through the tunnel to the cathedral, rolling them on a mover's dolly. They were all in the room before the sun began to rise.

Rose bent, leaned her shoulder against the shelf unit to tilt it, gripped it with her hands and paused for a second. She thought of Henry as she had found him, pale and silent, lost to her.

When she lifted, the shelf unit wanted to fall forward away from her, but she bent back and gradually the weight came against her body, and with her arms at the limit of their strength, the muscles beginning to shudder, she slid the wooden frame carefully into its place.

It was done, one more step. She would complete her task before the poignant useless words were spoken over Henry's corpse.

Shortly after seven, a car drove into one of the small parking lots at the back of the cathedral. Tom Chapman, the cathedral sexton, climbed out and carefully locked the car behind him; he kept the ring of keys in his hand to let himself in a small side door of the church hall where he saw rows of straight chairs left after a meeting the night before, but instead of stopping to replace them in stacks where they belonged, he went through the body of the church and down to the basement to the room where the cleaning supplies were kept. He put on the kettle and waited for his assistant to arrive. They had to dust all the pews and the chancel in time for the bishop's funeral at ten-thirty. By the time the kettle had boiled, Bill was on hand, and without conversation, the two men drank their coffee and set to work. They had about a third of the pews dusted when the dean, an early riser at any time, and today especially concerned that the funeral go off without a hitch, appeared through a door in the south transept and looked around him. He was a slender, rather elegant man with a seamed and worried face. In his pocket were notes for the short eulogy he intended to deliver at the service. He stood at the chancel steps, as if rehearsing the whole funeral in his mind. He looked all round him, saw no signs of imminent catastrophe and left the building.

Rose turned the last shining steel screw, set in place the shelf that concealed the screw head and stepped down from her wooden stool. She was done. Her head was throbbing, and her back and shoulders ached, but the wooden shelves and cupboards were completed. The lines were simple and, she hoped, attractive enough that if the building survived five hundred years, her work would still be found sufficient, like that of some anonymous mediaeval joiner who had created a set of cathedral choir stalls from which holy voices had risen for hundreds of years. Soon enough Rose would be gone from the diocesan office; there was no place for her there now the bishop was dead, and once she had disappeared, it would be only days or weeks until she was forgotten, until no one quite remembered who had worked and polished the wood that furnished this little room.

She swept the floor, leaving the little heap of wood shavings and brick dust and discarded screws in the corner of the room. Chappie could finish. From the pocket of her carpenter's apron, she took a clean cloth and gave the wooden surfaces a last rub, then turned to go. She was covered with dirt and sweat, and her hair was gritty with the plaster and brick dust that had fallen as she drilled into the walls.

Leaving, she paused at the door for a moment, as if one more action must be performed, one more word spoken. She could hear noises, voices, from other parts of the building. The church was preparing itself for the funeral. She had made her funeral gift for Henry, but she felt no less empty for the achievement. Well, it had kept her busy, given the ache in her mind and heart and spirit a bodily home. Now she must tidy herself to appear in public – the bishop's efficient, pathetically devoted secretary seeing his body into the ground, surrounded by other worthies of the church.

Rose wanted to break something.

Just after nine o'clock, Gordon Budge, the cathedral organist and choirmaster, opened a small door in the wooden panelling near the organ and took his place at the organ console to practise. On the music rack in front of him, he spread his copy of the "Funeral Sentences of Henry Purcell." He would play these as a prelude while the mourners gathered. He switched on the blower, selected stops, and began, the building, which had been all light and air, suddenly resonant with the reverberations of sound.

While Gordon was practising, Elaine Heverson found a parking place on the street behind the church and slid her small car efficiently into it. She went in the back door of the church hall and along the corridor to the choir room. As chairman of the choir guild, she had to arrive early to make sure that the music was sorted and distributed, that the gowns were in order, and that the boys got themselves into a suitable state to appear by the beginning of the service. It was she who had written the note sent home with each of the choristers asking their parents to arrange for the boys to be let off school for half a day to sing at the bishop's funeral, and she had phoned all the mothers the night before to remind them. In her purse was a list of the boys who would be on hand for the service.

A foolish thing, the human body, with its lumps and patches. Rose rubbed herself dry, scrubbed the wet hair on her head until the scalp hurt. She stood in the small bathroom of the bishop's apartment, uneasily surrounded by the traces of the man's life — a safety razor, toothbrush, a few medicaments — catching glimpses of her naked body in the small mirror over the sink.

When she had returned from her apartment in the middle of the night, Rose had brought with her a dress in case there wasn't time to get home and change, and when she came out of the cathedral, hot and filthy, it had seemed a simple enough thing to come up here to get herself clean, but now she was all on edge. The sight of her naked body made her think of Henry's, assaulted by undertakers, encased for burial. Two bodies among the millions. How many had died at the same moment as the bishop, how many been born? One of Chappie's compilations of facts would surely tell.

Rose pulled on some clothes, rolled the dirty work-clothes into a bundle and put them in a plastic bag to be set aside in the drawer of her desk . . . combed her hair into place. She was ready.

She wasn't, of course, never would be, ready to acknowledge him lost to her forever. Faithless, faithless, Rose. Not lost. *I go before you to prepare a place for you.* Well, perhaps, who was to know, but as Rose opened the door and stood in the bedroom where she had last seen him, that pale empty face, she felt herself alone on some vast plain of space and time, mute and in dread.

After the funeral, she supposed, it would fall to her to empty the little apartment of the bishop's possessions, see them thrown out or given away. Perhaps then she would weep. Now she was as dry and hard as a rock on that vast plain.

On the dresser across from the bed were Henry's photographs. She'd seen them a dozen times but never looked at them, the two photographs in silver frames. Now she looked. One was a young woman, dark, pretty, with an expression that was hard to fathom – frightened or petulant or sad – the face made more mysterious by the old-fashioned blouse and hair. The other was a photograph of a family, a man with a moustache, a dark suit and a straw boater, his wife, holding herself very straight and with one hand on the shoulder of each child – her sweet-faced daughter, and Henry, her son, perfectly recognizable even at that age, and smiling as Rose had known him to smile.

Rose put the pictures down.

By the window, still, was the straight chair where Ishakak had liked to sit, talking to Henry or himself in quiet guttural mumbles. The old man had gone back to the silence of the North, taking his gods with him.

The first person to arrive for the funeral was Annie Huberland. She was eighty-three years old and found it difficult to walk as quickly as she once had, but she refused to use taxis, except in the very worst weather. So she had set out from her house very early, but the walk to the cathedral was downhill, and on this fine day she had moved more quickly than she expected. She was startled to enter the building and find herself alone. She stepped slowly up the centre aisle to the pew where she had sat for eighty years, unfolded the kneeler, and with some difficulty bent her arthritic knees to pray. During the long history of her life, dozens of cathedral clergy had come to minister here and then gone away, the words of the liturgy passed from mouth to mouth, but this bishop was a favourite of hers, and she found it easy to think prayerfully of him. By the time she lifted her head and opened her eyes, a few others had begun to arrive. Her friend Mary Marshall sat beside her, nodded and knelt.

A few civic dignitaries were beginning to appear, some of them uneasy in the cathedral, unsure what was required. They found their way to pews and sat stolidly.

The sound of the organ covered the shuffling of feet, the mumbled words.

A handsome young server in a black gown lit the candles and set the clergy prayer books in order.

Finally the choir filed in to the stalls and sat, and from a small door in the north transept, Elaine Heverson appeared, her work done, and sat in a pew beside her husband, Robert, a ruddy, handsome man with bright blue eyes.

Since the bishop had no family, the front pews were taken by some of the clergy and diocesan staff who had been close to him – his secretary, Rose Goodwin, Frank Neal, his executive assistant, along with Frank's wife, Ruth, Canon Stanley Butts and his wife Mildred, Curwan and Marjorie Brant. Edgar Worral and other members of the diocesan executive sat one row behind them.

After these men and women had taken their places, the choir stood and sang Purcell's "Thou Knowest Lord the Secrets of Our Hearts." Then the whole congregation came to its feet as the dean's ringing voice was heard from the back of the church.

" 'I am the resurrection and the life, saith the Lord:

he that believeth in me, though he were dead, yet shall he live: and whosoever liveth and believeth in me shall never die.' "

He paused and spoke again.

" 'Let not your heart be troubled: ye believe in God, believe also in me. In my Father's house are many mansions: if it were not so, I would have told you. I go to prepare a place for you.' "

After a momentary pause, he spoke the third of the introductory sentences.

" 'I know that my Redeemer liveth, and that he shall stand at the latter day upon the earth.' "

He spoke the last sentence.

" 'We brought nothing into this world, and it is certain we can carry nothing out. The Lord gave, and the Lord hath taken away; blessed be the name of the Lord.' "

The coffin began to move up the aisle. Many of those who saw it pass by were surprised at the escort of military pallbearers.

As the coffin reached the chancel steps, one of the clergy carried out the bishop's mitre and crozier and laid them on top of the wooden box, and the choir began to chant, the pale voices of the boys rising into the stone vault on the building and resonating softly.

Rose was surrounded by enemies. She wanted to flee. Even the gentle face of Stan Butts was foreign, hostile. The dean, standing in the pulpit, was talking about the bishop, delivering a eulogy, but she could get no grip on what was being said. She had lost her interpreter.

"Henry was an exceptional man," the dean was saying. "A military guard of honour is here as testimony to his bravery as a military chaplain in the Second World War. In 1945, he was awarded the Military Cross for valour, a rare decoration, and one even rarer among military chaplains. As the men of the Canadian Army moved through Holland, our bishop, who like every chaplain went into battle armed only with his faith, became celebrated among his men for the bravery with which he served them, giving comfort, saving lives on more than one occasion. For risking his own life to save two men trapped in a burning tank which was still under enemy fire, he was awarded the Military Cross."

Rose hadn't known this. Another secret. Henry had never mentioned it. So much she didn't know, the world so full of secrets. In the red glow of a stained glass window, she saw the tank, burning with the fire of hell and Henry, young and radiant, walking into the flames. There was his face, and he smiled at her, and the enemies were gone, the voice of the dean far away. Then she wasn't frightened, nor any longer angry. She was staring, entranced, at a patch of light on the crimson carpet in front of the altar rail, a patch of sunlight that shimmered like water; she was staring into it as if Henry had brought her here to see it and promised that it contained the secrets of all the world.

After the benediction, the guard of honour rose to accompany the coffin in a slow march as it was wheeled down the aisle on its trolley by two men in dark suits.

The organ played as the choir filed out and the congregation began to emerge from the narrow pews into the aisles for departure, in small groups, alternately moving and waiting, like men and women attempting to leave a crowded train, their impatience to be gone only partly disguised by their politeness among strangers.

Those who would accompany the body to the grave made their way to cars for the journey. The others, who found themselves outside the church in the bright summer sunlight, struggled a little as they tried to cast off, but not too swiftly, too indecently, the aura of funeral solemnity to return to a tone of being more suited to ordinary life. Inside the church, a server appeared to snuff the candles then disappeared. His postlude finished, Gordon Budge folded his music and made his way out, and in a few minutes the cathedral was left empty. The bright light of noon, coming through the stained glass windows, and the pebbled glass around the dome, hung in the air and made all the surfaces gleam. On the walls at each side of the church, brass and marble plaques commemorated those who had been part of the cathedral's long history — the original architect and builder, the donors, earlier bishops, church wardens, a young army officer who had come from a local family and gone west to be killed in the battle of Batoche fighting against Riel, a fourteen-year-old boy who had drowned while attempting to save the life of a friend.

Brightness hung in the air, filling and defining the high spaces, circling the tall pillars of the nave, dropping in rich colours through the windows of the chancel. The dome was a small, perfect sky. The bishop's chair stood empty, the grain of the polished oak with its ragged seams soaked in the gentle contained luminescence of the church interior.

The building was drenched in stillness.

Sunlight fell, the light of noon, of evening, of morning, the blinding sun of summer, the dim, cloud-clotted light of November, pale moonlight that hovers over snow in the dead cold of a winter night. The light of noon, fields in the heat of summer, foxtail barley, buttercups, chicory, daisies, Queen Anne's lace. A ray of sunlight from an open window falls in a pool of brilliance just in front of the brass communion rail where generations of worshippers have knelt. The patch of light moves, in a stately dance, across the crimson carpet. Through the open doors of the church sound the calls of birds who will sing and mate and raise their young in nests of grass and die. The sun passes across the infinite spaces of the sky, and the ray of sunlight vanishes from the church floor.

Light and darkness, summer and the hard winter. A sound of wind in leaves, like the rapid turning of pages, as if one turned the pages of a scripture seeking answers for all the world's unanswered questions, the pages turning, the leaves, faster and faster, the wind rising, the questions multiplying, the hard winter darkness thickening the air like smoke, then slowly light returns, the one day of the year on which the rising sun strikes the east window and throws its light on the altar.

The white horse comes slowly up the centre aisle towards the sanctuary, his ears pricked up, moving tentatively, eyes wide, his hoofs knocking against the stone floor at each step, the daylight like a silver oil on his white coat and mane. Head turns, the ears flick, searching for possible danger in this great stone barn in the middle of deserted fields. He is enclosed, imperilled. He whinnies softly, the nostrils flare. The body is lifted high on the delicate legs, poised, ready for flight. Nothing stirs. The sun illuminates a stained glass rendering of the risen Christ.

The white horse turns his head, as if hearing a sound somewhere in the distance, wind altering its direction among the leaves. Suddenly jittery, he trots down the aisle and out the door.

Vanishes.